Patricia

100 Years into the Future

Conway Cates

ISBN: 978-0-9977322-3-8

Table of Contents

Preface vii

The Beginning .... - 1 -

Patricia .... - 17 -

A New Start .... - 39 -

30 Years into the Future .... - 51 -

Randy's Trip .... - 73 -

100 Years into the Future .... - 83 -

Henry .... - 101 -

Kidnapped! .... - 119 -

Freedom .... - 141 -

Las Vegas .... - 159 -

Again? .... - 173 -

The Roundup .... - 185 -

Wrapping Up .... - 215 -

A Word from the Author .... - 222 -

Preface

My name is Conway Cates. The following story was related to me by my long time friend, Gregory Allen Gray. The story is told in Greg's own words starting in the following pages. I have prompted him for details and helped outline the conversations he was able to recall.

Greg's father and I became friends in high school and joined the Air Force together. I later studied some journalism in college, and once wrote an unpublished book, so he contacted me for help with writing his story.

It has taken us years to complete this project. I had a family and a day job, so I didn't always have the necessary time to dedicate to this. Greg would remember more and more as we went along. He would send me emails and occasionally fly back to Ohio to work with me for a weekend.

Greg met someone and married again, spending a lot of time with her and their young foster children, so we were delayed further. He has steadfastly insisted that this writing become a book. It is essential to his story as you will discover while reading.

The Beginning

My name is Gregory Allen Gray. I am five foot eleven with black hair, blue-grey eyes, and I weigh about 185 pounds. I am probably considered by most people to be a good looking guy.

In March of 1995 I won the California SuperLotto Plus jackpot. It totaled more than thirty-six million dollars. There was another winner and we split the pot.

I took the lump sum option which radically reduced the amount I would receive. Of course, it wasn't all mine. Uncle Sam took 24 percent withholding first. My attorney got his. I gave some to friends and family. It left me with seven million, eight hundred thousand dollars and change. Tough luck, eh?

I was 28 years old and working for Ma Bell at the time. That's what some older employees called the Pacific Bell Telephone Company. Others called it PacBell. I was a teletypewriter repairman working in the Los Angeles area. My job was to repair the old teletype machines the deaf used instead of telephones.

I was one of very few technicians in the country who were trained to maintain the old machines. There were two of us in the Los Angeles region working from the same office. There was only one other technician in Southern California. She worked out of San Diego. I met her one time at a training meeting.

Teletypewriter Corporation created remarkable machines. Their KSR 28s and ASR 33s were a mainstay of wire communication for many years. KSR meant Keyboard Send and Receive and ASR stood for Automatic Send and Receive. They were electro-mechanical marvels intricately designed to generate an electrical signal over a telephone line. The signal was received by a remote machine and was converted to a typewritten message by an electromagnetic relay and mechanical systems. Essentially, it was an automatic typewriter driven by a coded telegraph signal. They were ancient and on the verge of extinction due to smaller facsimile machines—they were once desk sized—and the personal computer.

My job was in jeopardy. Many companies once used the teletype machines but upgraded to fax machines and computers. Only poor or older deaf persons used the KSR's. There were more than four hundred still in use in Southern California. Looking back and considering today's technologies, that seems ridiculous. However, computers and fax machines were only recently in common use by small business and starting down in price.

Finding parts to repair the engineering masterpieces was becoming more and more difficult. We often ordered custom parts from a local machine shop.

I enjoyed working on the teletypewriters. I didn't enjoy the fact that they were slow and archaic as communication devices. At 110 characters per minute, they couldn't compete with the latest graphical transmissions of the PCs and fax machines.

Not that I would have lost my job—just my vocation. I would have been cross trained to do something else. I wasn't looking forward to it. I loved the mechanical side of my trade. The electrical side was less interesting to me at the time. Little did I know how interesting electronics would become.

That week before my lottery win was unusual in many ways. I broke things off with my latest girlfriend, Barbara, on Sunday. It was a little devastating. I was unable to sleep that night.

Monday. Blue Monday. I managed to make it through the workday. I picked up a bottle of Bacardi and a six pack of

Coca-Cola on the way home. I didn't drink much liquor, as a rule. That night I did.

Tuesday. Terrible Tuesday. Hangover. Worked anyway—barely. I crashed Tuesday evening when I got off work and hit the bed. I finally slept.

On Wicked Wednesday I wrecked my car. Dumb. I pulled out in front of a blue Camaro traveling south on La Cienega Boulevard. Fortunately, there were no injuries except my pride, and Julie, my precious red Mazda. She was only two months old. I got a ticket and settled for a Pontiac Grand Am from the rental company while my car was being repaired.

Thursday. Thrashing Thursday. One of the busiest days of my life. I handled five trouble calls, replacing each machine and leaving the repairs for later or the next day. One trouble call per day was the norm for me, though I occasionally got two. My area was north, east, and northwest of Los Angeles. Bill Edwards, my alternate technician, was usually assigned to outlying areas south and southeast of Los Angeles.

The real trouble call came about three that afternoon. My friend, Carl Swanson, got himself shot in Watts. What the heck was he doing in Watts, anyway?

I spent the evening at Centinela Hospital comforting Carl's wife, Robin. She was a petite woman, maybe five foot two, with mousy brown hair down to her waist. Her brown eyes usually sparkled, but that day they were not so bright. She was only-so-very-slightly overweight and looked cuddly on most other evenings. That night, she looked worried.

I met Carl while repairing his deaf sister's teletypewriter nearly eight years before, shortly after my initial training. He was stout with brown hair, five foot ten, and deep blue eyes that seemed to snap when he was angry. He was always wisecracking and that made the repair visit to his sister's house enjoyable.

When I ran into Carl later in the week at a night club in Redondo Beach, we started talking and eventually became close friends. We often went to the desert to go hunting for jack rabbits. Occasionally we tried to play golf. We went to Las Vegas twice for a weekend getaway before he married Robin.

Carl worked as a welder for a fabricating shop in El Segundo. He was mechanically inclined, giving us something in common. We worked out mechanical challenges together several times over the years.

Carl married Robin five years earlier. I was his best man. Robin was an executive secretary at Northrup Grumman. Northrup Aircraft had merged with Grumman Corporation the previous year.

Carl came out of surgery sometime after midnight.

I asked, "What happened?"

"My boss offered the afternoon off with pay to make a delivery to the Watts Towers Art Center. I agreed since it would only take an hour or so. Afterwards, I stopped at a service station on Imperial for gas. I decided to go into their store for a soft drink and a loaf of bread before getting on the freeway. I stumbled into a robbery. I got shot as I lunged for cover when the two robbers started shooting on their way out of the store. Smashed my loaf of bread when I landed on it. Luckily I hadn't paid for it yet."

"At least you haven't lost your sense of humor. Maybe when the drugs wear off?"

Robin laughed. Carl laughed and then frowned in pain.

I said, "Why did they bring you clear over here to Centinela Hospital? Martin Luther was closer, wasn't it?"

"'Cause I asked them to. This is where my doctor practices. They said it would cost more, but I didn't care. The store's insurance pays for it anyway."

It was after midnight before I left the hospital. I was tired and readily fell asleep, but then I tossed and turned a lot.

Friday. Frantic Friday. It was the second busiest day of my life. I got a call at four thirty in the morning. It was Robin calling from the hospital. She said, "Carl has taken a turn for the worse. He is back in the operating room."

"I'll be right there."

I was at the hospital by five AM. I questioned Robin as soon as I saw her, "What happened? I thought he was doing well."

"The doctor came by, looked at the wound, and said Carl needed to go back to surgery. He said there were lead remnants left in the wound and they need to get them out. I called you as soon as they took him."

"Okay, I guess they know what they are doing. At least I hope so."

"Me too."

There was nothing I could do but wait with Robin. I dozed off in a chair.

Robin shook me awake. "He's back. They think they got all of it this time. They took x-rays to be sure."

We watched while they wheeled Carl into his room and got him into bed. He was recovering from the anesthesia. He lazily opened one eye and looked at me. "Howsha—howsha doin'?"

"The question is—how are you doing?"

He blinked several times, shook his head as if trying to wake up, and then answered with a dreamy style of voice, "I think I'm gonna fly to work tomorry. Right now, my wings feel heavy."

Robin leaned over him and whispered. "Get some rest, honey." Carl closed his eyes and his head fell slowly to one side.

Robin looked at her watch and then at me. "What time are you supposed to be at work? It's almost seven thirty."

"Eight o'clock."

"There's nothing you can do here. Go to work."

"Okay, bossy."

I leaned over and kissed her on the cheek. "Take good care of him."

"I will. Git goin' or you'll be late."

I timed it. Thirteen minutes' drive to the Hawthorne Central Office. I began repairing the machines I had brought back to the office. I got a new trouble call about ten fifteen and I had to drive up to Camarillo. It was an hour and half drive. Since I was going that far, I took a working machine with me to replace the troubled one.

I bought the lottery ticket when I stopped for gas and a Pepsi on the way back to the office. I probably wouldn't have if the jackpot hadn't been so high.

Buying a lottery ticket was not usual for me. When the lottery first started in 1984, I bought tickets each week even though I was a minor. The prospect of winning was intriguing, but seemingly futile. I eventually gave up the idea of becoming instantly rich. I didn't know what I would do with it anyway.

I continued repairs in the afternoon and asked Bill Edwards to help with an errand the next morning. He agreed. Although I had not slept much the night before, I spent the part of the evening at the hospital. I crashed hard when I finally got to bed. Carl? He had a sore butt.

Things got back to normal on Saturday. I awoke early and played golf at PGA West on my computer part of the morning. I was a better golfer using the computer program than I was for real. It was relaxing. I drove over to Carl's house and Bill Edwards picked me up about ten thirty.

I visited Carl in the afternoon. He was sleeping. I woke him up. I said, "Feeling better?"

"Not quite as bad as yesterday. Still hurts even with the painkillers and they make me sleepy. They say I can go home later today. Wow. I am sleepy. These pills have quite an impact."

"Great. Glad to hear you're going home. Bill Edwards and I just got back from Watts. We went down to the service station and brought your pickup home. I also rented a cot and set it up in your living room. I'll come by tomorrow afternoon. Let Robin know, will you?"

"Yeah. She left to go home to shower and change clothes. I'm gonna go back to sleep now." He closed his eyes.

"Okay. I must have just missed Robin. Tell her I said to hang in there. See you tomorrow."

Saturday evening, I went to a local night club looking for my hundred and first girlfriend. I enjoyed myself, but no luck. At least I didn't get drunk.

On Sunday I visited Carl at his house. Robin and I teased Carl and we never laughed quite so much—until she asked about Barbara.

I said, "All I can say is—it's over."

"Oh, I'm so sorry."

"It happens. I don't know why it happens to me so often. I will survive."

Carl interjected, "Sorry, buddy. You'll find the one someday."

Robin chimed in, "That's right. You can't rush it. Just be yourself and she will come along eventually."

I frowned and nodded.

Monday. Money Monday. That was some day. The lottery drawing was on Saturday, March 18. I was at work when I read in the LA Times that there were two winners, one who bought a ticket in Camarillo and one in Sacramento. My ticket was at home.

I arrived at my apartment in Manhattan Beach around five thirty that evening. It was a two-bedroom second story apartment in a residential neighborhood a few blocks from the beach on Crest Drive. I used the second bedroom for my computer desk and for extra storage. I called it my office.

After changing into a pair of shorts, I laid down on the couch in the living room to watch television. I liked to watch the evening news when I could. One of the top stories was that the lottery winners had not come forward. I decided to find my ticket and check the numbers. I hastily wrote down the numbers as they were displayed on the television screen.

I found the ticket on my bed stand and returned to the living room to check it. I'm sure my eyes expanded to the size of golf balls as I read the numbers to myself—five times. I was astonished—and scared.

Does that surprise you? I didn't know how I was going to handle the situation or what I might do with the money. I would probably like a new car after Julia was wrecked, but that was all I really wanted or needed. I didn't know what the process would be to turn in the ticket.

I called Carl. "Hey, Carl, I'm the big lottery winner they're looking for!"

"Sure. And you're going to give me half—right?"

"I'm serious, Carl. I'm one of the big winners. I bought a ticket when I went to Camarillo the other day for work. What do you think I should do now?"

"You are serious, aren't ya?"

I guess I could understand his disbelief. It had taken me more than an hour to call him. I had paced throughout the apartment while thinking it over.

"Absolutely, Carl. I don't know what I need to do. Any ideas?"

After a moment of silence, Carl replied, "Hell, no! Not a single real idea off the top of my head. Hey, Robin!"

"Carl! Don't tell anyone yet! Can I come over? Oh, I guess you can tell Robin, but don't tell another soul until we can talk!"

"Hell yes, ya can come over! How soon will ya be here?" He was getting excited.

Carl and Robin lived in a two-bedroom house in El Segundo on Maryland Street. He bought the house shortly after their wedding. Robin planted a couple of small trees and lots of flowers to dress up the place. It held a certain old-fashioned curb appeal, lacking only a white picket fence.

I was there in sixteen minutes. An airplane was landing at LAX—the Los Angeles International Airport. This location was near the south runway, which was the one they used for most flights. I once counted seven planes landing in ten minutes. The north runway was used for larger aircraft.

I pulled into the driveway and went past the house to a parking pad in the rear. I left the car and headed for the kitchen door. The door opened before I got there.

Robin shouted over the sound of the plane. "Get the hell in here and tell us all about it!" She hugged me with delight as I walked in. "I'm so happy for you!"

I frowned.

She asked, "What's wrong? Aren't you happy?"

"Right now, I'm more afraid than happy. Of course, I'm excited, but I don't know how to handle this. It's scary. Is Carl still on the cot in the living room?"

She smiled. "Naturally. He's not walking yet."

We went into the living room. Carl was lying on his stomach in front of the television. His hair was ruffled, and a sheet was thrown over his backside. He was watching over his shoulder for us to come in.

"What the hell took ya so long?"

"Oh, I stopped by the market and the mall on the way. Also, I got stopped by a cop for going too slow."

"Ha-ha. Okay, let's talk about these millyuns ya won."

I explained how I discovered I had won. We talked until shortly after midnight about what to do and how to do it. We determined no one else should know until I turned the ticket in to the lottery people. We decided I should consult a tax attorney before making any final decisions about what to do with the money.

I resolved to give Carl and Robin a hundred thousand dollars per year. I imagined that meant putting two or three million dollars into a trust fund or some similar investment.

I decided not to quit my job yet. I thought about whether to share some with my co-workers. I decided to do something for them, but not a lot.

We all went to bed. I stayed at Carl's house on the couch. I couldn't sleep that night. I was daydreaming all night long.

I called off work the next day. I put the ticket in a safety deposit box at the bank. I went to see an attorney and then stopped at Carl's house. We discussed what the attorney told me. Then we talked more until bedtime. I didn't sleep much that night, either.

I went to work on Wednesday. I turned in my two weeks notice, telling my boss that I would be taking an extended vacation, long overdue. He tried to pry further, but I stopped him short by telling him I would probably be back in a month. I told him I needed a rest.

He started to complain he wouldn't have anyone to do my job. I reminded him I seldom did much anyway, and Bill Edwards could easily handle what I did. They were wondering what to do with both of us for months.

It was a slow day, no trouble calls. I spent an hour and a half fixing the machine I replaced on Friday. The day dragged on and on. I was anxious to tell everyone I won the lottery, but my attorney advised me to keep quiet until everything was set.

Slowest day of my life. Longest day of my life. I decided not to go through it again. I told my boss I wouldn't be back except to pick up my final check. Everyone wished me well at quitting time.

I spent the evening at Carl's again. I needed to talk with someone. Carl and Robin were ecstatic. By now they understood my fears. Carl gave notice at his job. So did Robin. I changed my mind and decided they should have two hundred thousand a year. They were a comfort, and very supportive for several years.

I changed my mind about many things that week. The ideas what to do with the money came and went. There were things I was going to buy and then decided not to. There were charities I was going to support and then decided not to. There were investments I was going to make and then decided not to. My mind was churning. It was Friday morning before I finally got some sleep, two hours before the alarm went off.

I set up a trust to receive the funds at the Bank of America. That way I could maintain some privacy about where I was. The trust could distribute the monies I designated for Carl and Robin, some other friends, and my family members. My attorney told me the lottery commission would not want to distribute the income for me unless it was equally to everyone. Maybe he was right, maybe not, but I followed his advice. It gave me more control for the future.

I gave notice to my landlord. There wouldn't be any way I could continue living there, according to my attorney. California would not allow me to be an anonymous winner. Salespeople and reporters would be hounding me.

I had my telephone service discontinued. We then had an unlisted number installed at Carl's house using his name. I would stay with Carl and Robin until I found a new place to live. I moved everything I would be needing. I gave away a lot of stuff to the Salvation Army.

The media was in a frenzy. It was nightly news the Camarillo ticket holder had not come forward. The Sacramento winner had turned in his ticket on Tuesday. Some reporters were speculating the winner was out of state and didn't know he or she was a winner. Rumors abounded. We were tickled by it all, but I knew I would eventually have to face them. I wasn't looking forward to it.

I turned in the ticket on Friday morning. The lottery people were nice. They made me sign papers, get pictures taken, sign more papers, and sign more papers. Someone told the reporters outside I was there. Interview after interview. Unavoidable. The most asked question was, "What are you going do with the money?" I wasn't sure.

They wouldn't let me leave! I escaped out a restroom window around four in the afternoon. My attorney blocked the door to keep them out while I was inside. I made it to my rental car before two of them saw me and gave chase. I managed to lose them quickly.

I would have to go through it all again. One of the conditions of winning was to make a commercial for the lottery. And the press would be there.

I found a pay phone to call the friends and family who were to receive money. I didn't want any long-distance tracing to find me. None of them were told until I turned in the ticket. That's one reason the media didn't know anything about me. Now they would be inundated with publicity. I wanted to be first to warn them.

When I tried my parent's house in Marietta, Ohio, the line was busy. It took nearly an hour of constant trying to get through. The reporters found them first. Damn them! It spoiled my surprise and left me feeling sick about not telling them beforehand.

Mom and Dad were naturally upset with me for not warning them. They ultimately agreed to accept my gift. They left the house for a while to avoid reporters. They now live in Florida near my brother and his wife.

Next, I called Barbara. She hung up on me the first time. I shouted, "You're a winner!" on the second attempt a few minutes later.

"Winner of what? Another heartbreak?"

She cried when I told her it was ten thousand dollars, after I convinced her it was true.

"Why? Why?"

I tried to explain. She didn't believe me. Oh well. Her unbelief regarding a lot of things was the primary reason we weren't together. Trust issues.

Dad's parents were both deceased. My grandmother on Mom's side was alive and living in a retirement community near Logan, Ohio. Mom told her I'd be calling. I often think of her delight when I let her know she would have no more money worries after a lifetime of struggling. She enjoyed the rest of her life immensely. She married again two years before she died of pneumonia.

My brother, George, was not at home when I called. I caught him at work on the evening shift. He was glad I caught him before the press did. He gave notice to his boss that evening.

By the time I returned to Carl's I was exhausted, but relieved. It was mostly over. I had a week to avoid everyone and relax. Robin offered me a rum and coke, which I gladly accepted. I went to bed shortly afterwards. I finally got a good night's sleep.

Saturday, I no longer needed the safety deposit box, so I asked Robin to return the key to the bank. The teller tried to find out who she was when he recognized my name.

I was the talk of the town already. Of course. It was all over the previous evening news and the morning papers. Robin took the long way home to make sure no one was following her.

Carl was reading the morning news when I walked into the living room Sunday morning. He was still lying on his stomach, although he could sit up for short periods by now. He began reading aloud.

"Mr. Gray had not told his parents of his good fortune. When contacted by this reporter, they were totally surprised."

My tone was sharp. "Who wrote that?" It irked me that they called my parents first. I asked the reporters at the lottery office not to contact my friends and family until the next day.

"Let's see. It was written by a Carol Hawk."

"I think I want to have a word with her."

I checked the phone book for the number of the news office. I picked up the telephone receiver and pushed some buttons. I asked to speak to Carol Hawk.

A female voice answered. "Hello."

"Ms. Hawk?"

"No. Ms. Hawk is out of the office today."

"Okay. Can you take a message for her from me?"

"Certainly, sir."

"I want you to tell her that Gregory Allen Gray, the recent lottery winner called. Tell her I hope she chokes on her dinner for calling my parents before I could talk to them. Let's see her quote that in the paper tomorrow."

I hung up before she could respond. I was sure there would be no mention of it in the next morning's paper, but perhaps she'd be kinder to the next person she writes about. I only partially hoped I wouldn't read of her choking on her dinner.

Carl thought my comments were a little weak. "You should have cussed her out."

"It wasn't worth that much effort, especially since it wasn't her on the phone. It felt better to have done something, though."

It was nearly six weeks before there was money available to me. The initial deposit into my new trust account was two hundred and fifty thousand dollars. The rest would come within sixty days. I transferred a hundred thousand to a new checking account. I gave Carl a check for fifteen thousand dollars so he could pay off some bills.

I gave my eight fellow workers of many years five thousand dollars each. I felt it was enough to help each out, but not so much they would all quit work, leaving the company short. Besides, just because they worked with me was not reason enough to adorn them with too much money, according to my attorney. There were a few other friends I gave one-time cash gifts.

I planned to buy a new car, some clothes, and find a house. I did.

The car? A Corvette convertible. I had always wanted one. It was baby blue and a special edition with all available options.

The clothes? The best I could find on Rodeo Drive in Beverly Hills. I spent nearly $3000 for a tailor-fit Giorgio Armani suit and shoes, just for the thrill of it. I looked good in those clothes, but they weren't comfortable for all day wear. I rarely wore them after a while, opting instead for comfortable beach-style clothing.

The house? In Beverly Hills. I wanted to see how wealthy people lived. Taking advice from a real estate agent, I rented it with an option to buy after one year. I was glad I did.

I hired a staff of thirteen people. Three kept the house clean. Four were needed to keep guests happy and provide drinks or food. One was my secretary and managed the house staff. One managed estate security and his own staff of four.

It lasted seven months. Between nights out on the town and afternoon pool parties, none of which was without booze, I feared I was becoming an alcoholic. Fortunately, I never got into the drugs that were always available despite security staff efforts.

The new people in my life were mostly there for parties and freebies. I went through my second hundred girlfriends. Most women were pretenders, trying to be what they thought I might want them to be. Some wanted marriage, and some were impressed by fancy surroundings and wild parties.

Carl and Robin didn't like the scene in Beverly Hills. They moved to Scottsdale, Arizona after I was in the house for a few weeks. Carl plays golf nearly every day. Robin spends much of her time near the pool.

Okay, I tried it. It was thrilling at first but became boring. The parties and everything that went with them became tedious and expected of me. I wanted out.

I opted out of the contract on the house. I gave a lot of stuff away. I fired the staff. I spent more than nine hundred and sixty thousand dollars when all was said and done. All I had left were some clothes and the Corvette.

Patricia

When I left Beverly Hills, I wanted to be by myself for a while. I bought a little house east of Palmdale, California. It was out in the desert and deserted. A dirt road led away from a broken blacktop road and ended almost two miles later at my property, in a sand trap. The house hadn't been lived in for years.

I hired some workers from Lancaster to fix the place up. The road and sand trap were replaced with blacktop. They added three rooms and a garage. They updated the kitchen and bathrooms. They renovated the outside and installed a new roof. Since I was planning to purchase a small plane, a landing strip was built east of the house. A new heat pump and television satellite dish finished the renovation. Everything was done by the end of May.

I traded the Corvette for a four-wheel drive Chevrolet Blazer. It was far more practical for this environment.

I enjoyed the solitude after I moved in. My days entailed walking in the desert, taking flying lessons, and watching television. I became restless after about four weeks.

I began to visit a night club in Lancaster every couple of nights. I don't remember the name of the club. There were always a few airmen there from nearby Edwards Air Force Base. I was careful not to reveal my wealth to anyone. I soon became a familiar face there and was treated like everyone else.

I met Patricia Walling at the night club after a month and a half. She was being harassed by an overbearing Air Force lieutenant. I pretended to be her husband and stopped by their table.

"Was I supposed to pick up some milk for the kids on the way home, or were you gonna do that?"

They both looked up. He appeared a little upset at the interruption. She looked surprised.

She looked over at the lieutenant as she responded hesitantly, "I was planning to do it, but you can follow me as far as the store. Then I'll see you at home."

The lieutenant was angry. His response was gruff.

"You're married?"

She shrugged her shoulders and tilted her head. He left the table and went over to the bar.

She was appreciative. "Thanks so much. He was not taking no for an answer."

"No problem. Glad to help."

"Would you like to dance?" she asked.

"Sure."

I extended a hand. We danced the rest of the evening.

She was wonderful! Short blonde hair, five foot five, sparkling blue gray eyes, intelligent, caring, understanding, and full of frivolous fun! She was the secretary and bookkeeper for a screw machine company in Lancaster. I explained to her that I was on an extended leave of absence from the telephone company.

We had much in common on an emotional and intellectual level, as well as the obvious sexual attraction. We enjoyed dating for three months before I asked her to marry me.

I told her of my wealth only after she said yes. She was pleasantly surprised, to say the least. She jokingly chided me for hiding that information.

We were married in May of 1997. My parents, my brother and his wife, and Carl and Robin flew in for the wedding. I hadn't seen any of them for several months. Patricia's family was there as well. It was Carl's turn to be best man.

We went to Lake Tahoe for our honeymoon. The "Mile High Lake in the Sky" was beautiful. We enjoyed hiking and rowing a boat on the lake during the day, and gambling in the casinos on the Nevada side of the lake after dark.

We took a tour of the Ponderosa Ranch where I thought the old television show Bonanza was filmed. We discovered that wasn't entirely true—most filming within the ranch house was done in Hollywood. The ranch house at Lake Tahoe was a replica that did not include an upstairs. Still, it was an interesting tour.

We enjoyed the area. We stayed three weeks, although we planned only one.

We were ecstatically happy when we returned to the desert. We spent quiet evenings watching TV and playing board games. During the day, Patricia often went to town to see her friends and go shopping. I spent most of my days taking walks in the desert and reading a lot. We occasionally flew to Las Vegas for a few days.

It eventually became boring. That is when Patricia suggested I try to find some project to occupy my time and, perhaps, contribute to the betterment of mankind. If it involved moving, she would go with me anywhere, but she'd rather stay here near her friends and family.

I owned a computer. It was 1992 vintage with Windows 3.1. I had used it to draft parts for teletypewriters using a program called AutoSketch. I could also play games and make basic spreadsheets to manage my finances. Patricia had worked on a computer at her workplace and reported there were often problems with programs. Perhaps I could do better.

After much soul searching and discussion, I bought a new computer and starting learning how to operate the latest programs. The idea was for me to learn what programs were available. Then I could learn to write programs that were either better or not available in order to help people.

The computer I bought had eight megabytes of Random Access Memory (RAM), a one gigabyte hard drive, 15-inch monitor, 24-bit accelerated video card, cd rom, 28.8k modem, and Microsoft's Windows 95 operating system. It was one of the best available at the time.

There were many programs on the market, and I bought all the most popular. There were word processing programs, spreadsheet programs, financial programs, programs for drafting and graphics, and many game programs. Some of them were expensive. I spent over ten thousand dollars on programs in two months.

I hired a tutor to help me learn the systems. I found the computer so intriguing that I spent nearly every waking hour learning everything.

My tutor was a young man named Randy Martin who was attending Antelope Valley College. At nineteen, Randy was a good-looking kid. He was about six feet tall and maybe two hundred pounds. He had short brown hair and brown eyes. Mostly, he answered my questions and showed me what to do when I ran into trouble.

When Patricia would complain of the time I spent at the computer, I'd remind her it was her idea. She would kiss me on the forehead, tell me I was right, and I'd quit whatever I was doing to spend time with her. I told you she was wonderful!

One of my better ideas came to me while Randy was showing me how to use AutoCAD, a three-dimensional drafting program that was one of the most popular in industry. I thought it would be nice to be able to talk to the computer and have it draw the circles and lines as you wanted. It seemed like a simple concept. I just didn't have any idea how to do it.

Randy said. "You will need to have an advanced Artificial Intelligence program to do such a thing. To do something that complex, the AI program would probably have to be in a matrix. A matrix is several computers set up to operate with each other."

"Complex? Why is it all that complicated?"

Randy laughed before responding.

"Understanding what someone has said is difficult for a machine to compute. Intonations, voices, and accents alone would make it extremely challenging for a programmer, not to mention the English language itself. So many words have different meanings in different contexts. Some sound the same. For example, there is two, the number, which sounds the same as t-o-o and t-o. Yet a kid soon learns to understand such things with their own computer—their brain."

He paused, reflecting for a moment before continuing.

"The human brain is truly a marvel of nature's technology. We don't know enough about how the brain operates to duplicate what it does.

"A matrix configuration connects computer chips, called microprocessors, together in a system. The basic idea is to hook the chips together in such a way that whole instruction sets are split or pipelined and executed almost simultaneously."

I said, "That doesn't sound so complicated."

Randy laughed again. "Believe me. It is not easy."

That conversation stayed with me. Patricia said it was a marvelous idea. I would later attempt to do it.

It took me eight months to become reasonably competent at running all my programs on the computer. Randy became a friend of the family, often having dinner with us. We took him to Las Vegas with us a couple of times in the summer, although we usually preferred such times to ourselves.

We flew to Vegas every five or six weeks in the Piper Cub I purchased. Patricia and I loved going to stage shows and gambling at the casinos. She liked playing the slot machines. I preferred blackjack—a card game played against the house—the casino. I rarely bet more than ten dollars and tipped the dealers regularly.

It was just for fun, but I often won. Amazing. When I went there with Carl, and a lot less money, it seemed impossible to win. Now, in seven excursions I tracked on the computer, I averaged winning two hundred sixty dollars per trip. Patricia's average was ninety dollars. Randy won once for forty dollars. Beginners luck, we told him.

Then along came Eva Collins, a voluptuous, five foot three, red headed, green eyed coed Randy met at college. He began spending a lot of time with her and I was left studying on my own. He eventually married her.

We gave them a wedding present of twenty-five thousand dollars which they used to make a down payment on a house. He was extremely surprised, and grateful. They moved to her hometown of Bakersfield, California.

I began a self study of programming and learning computers inside out. I learned several programming languages with names such as Fortran, Cobol, Java, Pascal, and Python. I learned assembly languages and operating systems. I learned about bubble memories, Random Access Memory (RAM), and Read Only Memory (ROM). I read and learned all I could about matrix networking, pipelining, and everything bits and bytes.

I bought all the latest and greatest equipment as it came on the market, including a voice recognition device dubbed an Electronic Butler. It was invented by a magician from Valencia, California. He used it in his stage shows at the Magic Castle in Los Angeles to appear as if he could tell lights and other electrical items to do what he wanted them to do.

In August of 2003, Patricia and I flew to England to learn about their progress in speech recognition. It was the first stop on a tour of Europe that I had promised Patricia.

It was warm in London. We flew into Heathrow Airport on a Monday at four in the afternoon and took a taxi to the Mercer Street Hotel near the famed Piccadilly Circus. I wanted to take the underground railway, but Patricia objected. She felt it may be a little closed in for her comfort.

We decided to take a walk after checking in to the hotel. During our leisurely walk through Soho to find a restaurant, we approached two young women walking the other way.

I said, "Hello."

One young woman was lighting a cigarette and dropped a box of matches when I spoke. She blamed me. She spoke with a hackney accent as she picked up the box.

"Look there wot you've done!"

I apologized and we walked on. I looked back and saw her still glaring at me. Strange the things we remember.

We found an Indian restaurant named Punjab and decided to try it. Neither of us had ever eaten East Indian food, so we asked the waitress what would be good. She recommended a tasting meal. It was a seven-course meal with tiny servings of several Indian dishes. Most of the dishes were curried and therefore very spicy. We washed them down with a mango drink. We determined we liked Indian food but would probably not have it very often.

We went to a night club later that evening. We discovered it on the way back to the hotel. The cover charge was expensive, nearly fifty American dollars. Patricia noticed there were no singles in the entire place—that everyone was with someone. She said singles probably knew better, less expensive places to go. All the couples stayed to themselves, no one mingled, and few danced. Were Patricia not with me, I would not have stayed ten minutes.

We decided to play a little game. We talked to each other uttering noises that sounded like words with frenzied hand gestures.

I said it questioningly and cocked my head to one side. "Ka som da lessea do rin da?"

Patricia responded with animated hands. "Pom ra la mi los ridding!"

It wasn't long before we noticed everyone staring at us. More accurately, they were trying to avoid staring at us. We could imagine them trying to figure out what country we were from. It was fun. Patricia always made things fun.

Tuesday morning, we took a taxi to Kings Crossing railway station and traveled north by train. We checked into the Ashley Hotel in Cambridge.

I visited the University of Cambridge for the next few days. Patricia enjoyed wandering the meticulously manicured grounds and various museums nearby, and sometimes sunning by the river.

I met with people in the Information Engineering Division. I attended classes with their students for several days. My electrical knowledge and computer studies helped me understand much of what they were showing me. I remain grateful to the staff for their expertise and cooperation.

During late afternoon and evening hours, Patricia and I enjoyed various activities in and around Cambridge. We tried tenpins one rainy evening at the 28-lane Megabowl Centre. The next evening was rainy as well and we went to the Arundel House Hotel. It was next door to the Ashley and owned by the same people. We enjoyed a leisurely dinner in their conservatory.

Friday afternoon, we took a taxi out to the airport and rented a helicopter for a view of the countryside. Patricia loved the ride and decided we should trade the Piper in on a helicopter when we got back.

I responded, "Maybe we can get one in addition to the airplane, but the airplane is probably more useful for longer trips like those we take to Las Vegas."

"Those trips would be more enjoyable by helicopter. We could see so much more."

"I have my doubts about the practicality of that long a trip in a chopper."

Patricia said softly, "We can talk more when we get home." It was a sign the conversation was over.

On Saturday, we rented a square-nosed boat called a punt from Scudamore's. We punted on The College Backs, a middle stretch of The River Cam that flows through and around the college campuses. Punting involves using a five-meter-long stick to propel and guide the boat. It requires balance and practice to get it right. Patricia proved to be better at it than me.

I said, "This is so much fun! Let's do it again tomorrow."

"Okay, we can take a picnic and make a day of it."

On Sunday, we punted upstream on the Top River. I got too far to the outside on Dead Man's Bend and had to paddle back to shallower water. Patricia laughed her head off and teased me about it the rest of the day.

We enjoyed a noontime picnic on the riverbank at Grantchester. Then we took a walking tour through the picturesque village and sipped afternoon tea at the Orchard, just beyond the Grantchester Church. It was a great and tiring day. We returned to Cambridge in the evening.

I spent more time at the college on Monday and Tuesday. We took the fifty-minute train ride back to London Tuesday evening. We checked in to the Royal Lancaster Hotel, across from an entrance to Hyde Park. We were exhausted and slept well.

We walked through Hyde Park after breakfast the next morning. It was relaxing after the previous week's efforts. We enjoyed sitting on the bank at Serpentine Lake.

Later we found a Wimpy's hamburger restaurant and went in to have lunch. As we sat down and started eating, I became aware everyone was staring at us.

"Everyone is staring at us. Haven't they seen Americans before?"

Patricia looked around, "They are all eating with knife and fork while we eat with our fingers."

I glanced around the restaurant, "You're right. Do they think we are being crude or something?"

"I suppose so."

It seems the Brits have a thing about eating with the hands. It is considered unsanitary. Patricia's consensus was that hands and fingers were made before knives and forks. I had to agree.

We stayed in London a few days and saw many sights. We rode on the upper level of a double decker bus. We went through the Tower of London. We saw Big Ben, witnessed the changing of the guard at Buckingham Palace, and toured Windsor Castle, home to members of the royal family. Patricia was especially tickled by a sign at Windsor Castle that read, "Residents only allowed on the grass."

On our last evening we discovered a pub. It was the first place in London where we really felt welcome. We were greeted like long lost friends the moment we walked in. We drank beer with the locals and had a blast. Too bad it was our last night in town.

Patricia reluctantly consented and we took the underground train as we left the city. Eventually we emerged from underground and were rolling along through country fields to the North Sea. We sailed by steamship across the North Sea from Harwich to the Hook of Holland—a six-hour trip. Patricia got seasick when I leaned over the rail looking at the waves made by the ship. She couldn't do it and I teased her relentlessly.

The harbor at Hook of Holland was crowded with men of war floating on top of the water. I couldn't adequately explain what a man-of-war was to Patricia, so I looked it up on my recently purchased iPhone 3G.

"A Portuguese Man O' War looks like a jellyfish, but it is not a jellyfish. A gas-filled bladder keeps it floating on top of the water while tentacles up to fifty feet long dangle downward. The tentacles sting anything that comes in touch with them. These stings paralyze and kill small fish or other sea creatures, the prey, which is then eaten. Such stings rarely kill humans, but a single sting can be excruciatingly painful for fifteen to twenty minutes."

Northwest of the harbor was a beach jam-packed with swimmers and sun bathers. I remember wondering if they ever encountered a man of war. They were swimming about five hundred yards from the dock.

We traveled by train to Rotterdam and then on to Amsterdam. We heard many people say how great Amsterdam was, so we were extremely disappointed when we were greeted by fish smell as we left the train station. It was dark and the streetlights revealed lots of litter.

Patricia picked up a booklet in London that cataloged attractions, hotels, and eateries throughout Europe. When we found the street listed for the hotel she picked to stay in, we were further disillusioned. It was narrow and littered. It looked more like an alley than a street.

It was nearly nine o'clock in the evening. A small sign halfway to the next street indicated the hotel was through a small doorway.

Opening the door, we were confronted by Dutch-style stairs. Dutch stairs are widely regarded as the most dangerous type of stairs in the world for one simple reason—they are insanely steep and narrow.

We grudgingly climbed the stairs with our suitcases. I remember thinking that all the people who proclaimed Amsterdam's greatness would be stricken from our Christmas list.

We were greeted at the top of the stairway by the hotel owner. He stepped out of a doorway to our left. The doorway led to a small cafe. He invited us inside.

It was not a large room. There were two small tables to our left with a small dance floor and jukebox near the far wall. More small tables lined the far wall to the right. A fifteen-foot long bar was on our right with a swinging door for the bartender to use just inside the cafe entrance. People were seated on stools along the bar.

The moment we walked into the cafe; our opinion of Amsterdam began to change. The half-dozen people there greeted us warmly. There was a Canadian sailor, two college girls from the States, a German man, the hotel owner, and a French woman sipping cognac at the far end of the bar.

The juke box was playing, "In the year 2525, if man is still alive . . ." We joined the party.

The owner fixed us a free drink. He said, "The hotel is full tonight. However, if you are willing, there is a bed up in the attic you could sleep in tonight, no charge, and you can move into a room tomorrow."

We were tired and agreed. Everyone was so pleasant that it was another hour before we retired to the attic.

The owner led us down a long narrow hallway. Two more steep stairways at the rear of the building led to the attic room. It ran the length of the building. The attic was clean and neat. There was limited headroom as the rafters met in the middle of the room about seven feet high. Some stacks of sheets and blankets were along the side walls.

A double size bed was placed on a large rug at the front of the building. It was made up with clean linen and a quilt. It was kind of nice. Patricia would not have minded staying there our entire visit if the bed were bigger and the ceiling higher. Dutch stairs helped with the decision to move downstairs the next day.

The following day we enjoyed breakfast in the cafe. We checked into a room. Then we explored the city.

Further into town, we found a place called Dam Square where several vendors were selling a variety of things. It was a city block in size. I bought Patricia some balloons from one of the wagons.

Across from the square was a statue with wide circular steps leading up to it from all around. The statue, undoubtedly representing some famous Dutchmen, was centered on the flat top. We discovered it was a Nationaal Monument erected in 1952 as a memorial to those who died in World War II.

There were many young people around the statue, some of whom obviously slept there on the steps. Several of them carried backpacks and appeared to be American.

We explored the city further and took a ride in a glass covered boat through the canals. The boat was painted blue with white frames around the windows. There was a windshield in front of the boat captain. Along each side were vertical windowpanes curving over the top. The rear had a vertical pane like the windshield in front.

The views of the city were delightful from the boat. I enjoyed it except for the more noticeable fishy smell while we were in the harbor.

Patricia loved the ride. She said, "Look at the boats. There are almost as many boats as there are vehicles and bicycles. That one is big."

"So, I see."

"Look at that building. Such interesting architecture. I would never have thought of designing the windows like that."

She babbled like that all along the canals. I could only agree and laugh occasionally under my breath. It was interesting and fun.

We took an afternoon tour of the Heineken Brewery. After the two-hour tour of the facility, we were led into a cafeteria-style room. Some ladies brought pitchers of beer to the table. We were given an hour to drink all the Heineken beer we wanted. Patricia drank one glass and I drank several.

It took a minute for my eyes to adjust as we left the building into the afternoon sunlight around five o'clock. While I wouldn't say I was drunk, it took an hour or so, and a meal, for me to feel near normal again.

We took a walk through the Red Light District that evening. Prostitutes displayed themselves with brief clothing in picture windows along the street. A few of them stood outside their doorway and approached me without regard to Patricia. One said she and a friend could take care of both of us. I thought their prices were dirt cheap compared to American hookers. Patricia teased me for knowing that.

It was the people that made Amsterdam wonderful. They were warm and friendly. Most spoke at least some English. We spent three days there and hated to leave.

We traveled by train from Amsterdam to Frankfurt, Germany. The ride took roughly four hours. Along the way we saw several castles, usually situated above sheer cliffs. I promised Patricia we could tour one during our visit to Munich. Her book indicated there were at least three within a reasonable distance of the city.

We arrived in Frankfurt shortly after noon. There were a few minutes between trains, so we browsed shops in the train station. Some sold souvenirs. Some were selling food.

We snacked on a brätwurst sandwich with warm black Lowenbrau beer and thoroughly enjoyed it. Brät means finely minced meat and wurst is sausage. Patricia ate sauerkraut on hers and I put spicy mustard on mine.

We took another train on to München as it was spelled on the map. It was another three-and-a-half-hour ride. München, better known as Munich, is the capital of Bavaria—gateway to the Alps. Bavaria is a German state and describes the entire southeastern region of Germany.

While we had enjoyed our stay in Amsterdam, Patricia decided on better accommodations for our stay in Munich. We took a taxi from the train station and checked into the hotel Patricia selected from her book—the Hotel Bayerischer Hof. It was a five-star hotel with a lot of history.

My iPhone gave me the following information, "Bayerischer Hof was originally built due to the desire of King Ludwig I to have a first-class hotel in town. It opened in October of 1841 and when the first leaseholder died in 1897, it was purchased by Herrmann Volkhardt. It was almost destroyed by bombing during World War II. Hermann and his son rebuilt the property after the war ended."

Now it was owned by a fourth-generation granddaughter, Innigrit Volkhardt, who was modernizing the facility. An employee told us she was working on amazing plans for the hotel. It was mysterious enough to pique her interest, so Patricia wanted to know more. She was able to discover that Innigrit had the Blue Spa on the seventh floor built only three years ago. An interior designer named Axel Vervoordt was designing a restaurant garden with the ambience of an artist's studio. There were plans for a cinema in the future.

We were escorted to our room by a young man who ensured our luggage was safely transported with us. He opened the door, invited us in while handing us the key, and brought the luggage in behind us. He hung our hanging clothes in a closet and asked if he could do anything more. We declined the offer and tipped him.

Our room was located on the 3rd floor near the center of the hotel. It was a very nice room decorated in Pilati style. There was a king-sized bed, a desk and a seating area. It overlooked the "Promenadeplatz" and we could see parts of the inner city buildings.

After we checked into our room, we began to explore the city. It was early September and just after 5pm, so there was a little time before dark. In front of the hotel was Promenadeplatz, a grassy, tree-lined memorial park a block long situated between one-way streets. We crossed the park and went up a block. We turned left and then right toward the twin domes we saw from our hotel window.

The two domed towers were part of a church and extended more than three hundred feet above our heads. Patricia's book identified it as Frauenkirche, or Cathedral of Our Dear Lady. We walked to the front in a pedestrian area and stared upward for a couple of minutes.

Patricia got my attention, "Look behind you."

I turned and saw a sunken fountain with what looked like little tables scattered throughout the water. Some people were sitting around the area on the tiered stones leading down to and under the water.

"Wow. That's beautiful." I said.

"I know. I wonder what it's called."

We approached a couple sitting nearby and Patricia asked if they spoke English. The man spoke with a heavy accent.

"Ya. Some."

Patricia asked, "What is this place called?"

"Wasserpilz Brunnen. Englash is Water Mushroom Fountain. Is place to relax."

"Thank you. Nice place."

The man nodded and we walked away.

Patricia said to me, "It is a pretty place and seems like it would be a soothing place to sit and relax for a while."

We looked back at the domes for a minute and decided we would come back for a tour of the church. We walked up another street to the corner. This was not a through street, so we would have to turn.

The street sign told us this new street was Kaufingerstrasse. We learned later that during the Second World War, much of the Kaufingerstrasse was largely destroyed and finally demolished. In the1950s and 1960s many buildings were restored or rebuilt. Since 1972, it has been part of the pedestrian zone in the center of Munich. Since the 1990s, many buildings were undergoing modernization.

"Right or left, Lady Patricia?"

"We turned right last time. Let's go left this time."

We passed shop after shop and some larger stores. Our path led us directly to Marienplatz, a central square in the city center of Munich. It has been the city's main square since 1158. We spent an hour or so gazing at and taking pictures of the fabulous architecture.

In the middle of the square is a statue of the Virgin Mary on top of a high column and known as Mariensäule. There is an ornate fence around it with large lantern statues on each corner. The base below the statue is square and eight or ten feet high. There are angel warriors at each corner. About ten feet higher on a smaller base are four of what I might call angel faces—maybe cherubs. A round column rises another fifteen or twenty feet. It is one of several Marien statues located around Germany. She is considered Queen of Heaven. This one was erected in 1638 and had survived the war.

A city long building north of the statue houses the New Town Hall. Westward from the middle of the building is a clock tower. Five to seven stories above the street, the New Town Hall figurines created in 1908 re-enact events from town history every day on an ornate stage. It is known as the Rathaus-Glockenspiel. We spent half an hour taking pictures with Patricia commenting on virtually everything around the square.

We were hungry and dusk was evident. As we looked around, we saw several cafes and restaurants. One located almost directly across the square from the town hall caught our eye—Wildmosers. We dined on Weisswurst with hand-sized pretzels, sweet mustard, and of course, beer. We discovered Wildmosers was the birthplace of the famous Weisswurst, or white sausage. Delicious.

We took a leisurely walk, retracing our way back to the hotel. It had been a long and tiring day. We showered and slept well that night.

I awoke at seven-thirty the next morning. I fixed some coffee and looked through Patricia's book while she slept. After she awoke and got dressed, we discussed what and when to explore Munich.

We visited the Residenz München, an inner-city palace once inhabited by King Ludwig I when he was in town. We spent the morning there and Patricia insisted we see all ten courtyards.

Then we took a taxi to the Theresienwiese festival grounds, home of the famous Octoberfest that would open in two weeks. There were several gigantic tents built by beer brewers to serve thousands of people. There was even a balcony inside the biggest tent. It could serve more than 9,000 people. There were several smaller tents. It was difficult to see a lot because everyone was busy. They were setting up a carnival and getting ready for the big event. Patricia noticed how well the flowers and walkways were manicured.

On a hill at the west end of the grounds stood a large statue and a building with Greco-Roman style columns. The statue of Bavaria was added to the Theresienwiese in 1850 and is meant to symbolize Bavaria's power and strength. It depicts an Amazon woman holding the wreath of victory in her left hand. In her right hand is a sword and there is a majestic lion at her side. We discovered there were steps that would take you up to her head. It was a six-story climb, so we declined to go there.

Later that evening we went to a place listed in Patricia's book as the most famous tavern in the world, Hofbräuhaus. It may be the birthplace of Gemütlichkeit. One definition is cordiality, friendliness. We found it to be the friendliest place in town.

The Hofbräuhaus has several active groups of regulars and tables are often reserved for them. The oldest regulars` table had been held for more than forty-five years. We entered the Schwemme, their famous beer hall. Left of the entrance is a beer tap and beside that is a steinvault—a place where loyal customers can store their own stein, or German style mug.

They once brewed their famous Hofbräu München Bier right there in the Hofbräuhaus. Today, it is brewed on the outskirts of Munich and exported all over the world.

Everyone there was having a grand old time. We were seated at a table for ten in the Festival Hall on the second floor. We sat across from four young Australian women who were being entertained by a young German man sitting on our side of the table. He was a college student who delighted in practicing his English by talking with them and with us. He explained that English was a required school subject in his country. The differences in our accents versus the Australians was fascinating to him.

We dined on Schweinshaxe, which is roasted pig knuckle. It is crunchy on the outside and tender and juicy inside. A whole Schweinshaxe is enough meat for two people, so we each ordered the halb or half. It was served with Kartoffel Knödel which is a potato dumpling, Krautsalat and a Bier— Hofbräu original of course.

We had a ball that night despite being weary from the day's activities. We slept well after taking a taxi back to the hotel.

The following day we arranged a trip to tour Neuschwanstein Castle. It was the inspiration for Disney's Cinderella and Sleeping Beauty castles. The only way to see inside is on a 35 minute tour and no pictures are allowed. Since we made our reservations a little late, we had to wait nearly three hours for our tour. The 19th-century Romanesque Revival architecture is fascinating. It is a fabulous place to visit.

Here I am, rambling on about our trip to Europe. It was a cherished trip for me, so I wanted you to know about it.

I'll finish this part of my story by telling you we went to Paris, Madrid, Naples, Rome, and Athens. We relished special times and met special people in each city. We enjoyed various cuisines at out of the way places.

Did you know spaghetti in Italy is served without meat sauce unless you ask for it served separately? And lasagna noodles may be light green in color?

I got drunk in Athens, Greece. I tried to impress Patricia by climbing the hotel's eleven stories outside, from balcony to balcony in my underwear. Dumb! I cringe to think about it now. It was fortunate I was not arrested. Patricia was not impressed.

I wish I could remember the name of the hotel. The dinner we enjoyed there included a dish containing sliced chicken livers and seasoned rice. It was so delicious I have sometimes wondered about going back. I guess a little memory loss is what drinking too much can do for you.

We stayed only one night in Madrid. We didn't speak Spanish and most of the people we met didn't speak English. We decided most tourists probably studied Spanish before visiting.

The trip home took us to Paris. There a four-hour layover at Orly Airport before boarding a flight to New York. We seized the opportunity to lunch at a sidewalk cafe nearby. I remember the vision of Patricia sitting across from me with the Eiffel Tower in the background. Her hair was blowing softly in a light breeze. She was laughing much of the time. We always had fun together, no matter where we were.

The plane ride to Kennedy Airport in New York took more than eight hours and we learned to sleep while flying. Our earlier trip to London was aboard a supersonic plane called The Concorde and had taken only three and a half hours. We spent three days in New York City visiting various sights.

We flew From New York to Saint Louis and then to Las Vegas. We were tired and stayed the night in Vegas well off the strip at a hotel called Sam's Town. We usually stayed at Caesar's Palace but, without a reservation, we were unable to get a room along the strip. I personally thought the beds at Sam's Town were a little hard. Our room was near the bowling area and the noise was irritating at times.

I have often wished we had hired a plane to take us to Palmdale. Instead, we rented a car because we were tired of flying. Our car was hit head-on near the Nevada California border.

Patricia – 100 Years into the Future

A New Start

I awakened in the hospital six days after the accident. It took me a few moments to realize I was in a hospital. I buzzed for a nurse.

"What happened? Where am I? Where's Patricia?"

"Just a moment, sir, I'll get the doctor."

She left the room. Several minutes went by. My mind raced. Then a doctor entered the room followed by the nurse.

"Hello. How are we feeling?"

I was frantic. "Where's my wife, Patricia?"

The doctor looked at the nurse, then back at me. "I'm afraid we have some bad news."

He paused.

"Your wife died in the accident. It was immediate. She didn't suffer."

My initial incredulity soon gave way to a grief that overwhelmed me. The doctor instructed the nurse to prepare and give me a shot.

It was the next day before I was able to ask details about the accident. The details were sketchy. They didn't know much. They wanted to know more from me than I could tell them.

The man driving the other car died two days after the accident. His blood alcohol level was point two three, nearly three times the level needed to be declared legally drunk. Officers on the scene found two empty whiskey bottles in his car along with an unopened bottle that escaped breakage. They determined that his car was traveling 110 miles per hour and became airborne when it topped a small hill and flew into my vehicle. The man had lived alone in a small trailer near Riverside, California.

They used the jaws of life to extract me from the automobile after the accident. I was unconscious and bleeding from my forehead. My legs were trapped between the seat and firewall that had been pushed toward me by the engine. The steering wheel was bent and broken by my body.

My condition was critical when I arrived at the hospital in Las Vegas by helicopter three hours after the impact. I had a severe concussion on my forehead, broken ribs, bruised chest and heart, and internal injuries. Both calves and one forearm were broken.

My family and Patricia's visited me at first. Mom had taken a video of Patricia's funeral for my benefit, though some people had thought it tactless. Mom and Dad stayed nearby until I left the hospital, with Dad occasionally going back and forth to Florida keeping their affairs in order.

I underwent several operations and then spent four months recuperating in the rehabilitation wing. The doctors did a marvelous job. I was able to recover completely, except of course, for a broken heart. Mom and Dad rented a car to drive me home.

It was terrifying to return to our home in the desert without Patricia. My first reaction on entering the house was to bawl my eyes out. Mom and Dad tried to comfort me, but to no avail. After three days, I told them I needed some time to myself. They reluctantly headed back to Florida.

I missed her. The house was a lonely place while I was feeling that way. I spent several days walking in the desert during my waking hours. It relaxed me and helped rebuild my muscles and stamina.

During those first few weeks I cried myself to sleep most nights. I missed Patricia tremendously. I didn't leave the house except to walk. I had groceries delivered despite the extra cost. After the first month, I hired a maid to come in and clean the house once a week. By then things were in such a mess she charged double the first week.

Eventually I sat down at the computer and threw myself into my studies and projects. I ordered computer chips and parts from several mail order houses. I combined my experience with the Cambridge-learned knowledge I was somehow able to remember. I was able to fling together several different matrix designs. None of them worked to my satisfaction.

Browsing through some long-overlooked computer magazines in early 2005 brought my attention to a new computer chip. New to me at least. It was a 64-bit CPU chip. In 2003, 64-bit CPUs were introduced to the personal computer market. That could help me past the 4GB RAM access limits of the 32-bit processors. My RAM could now be a quadrillion byte memory. I found it exciting to bypass the limit holding me back.

I immediately left the house and drove to the computer store in town. The manager greeted me enthusiastically. "Where have you been?"

Naturally, he had missed me. I spent thousands of dollars there in previous years. I briefly explained what happened. He expressed way too much sympathy.

I asked about the 64-bit chip. He informed me it was introduced months before. He had two servers in stock that used the chip. I bought one on the spot. I placed an order for twelve dozen chips for experimenting.

It took a week for the chips to be delivered. I used the time to study their specifications and configurations. I designed a unique matrix for using them. When they arrived, I immediately began constructing the computer I had imagined.

My computer is housed in a four-foot wide entertainment center purchased from a furniture store. A 45-inch television screen fills the upper portion. Two nine-inch high chambers, two feet wide, are arranged down each side under the screen behind dark glass doors. I reinforced the bottom of the cabinet.

There are wooden doors on each side below the dark glass made to look like drawer fronts. The lower left contains my original circuitry. Storage and backup battery units are in the right side.

The construction included configuring several digital disc components used for added memory. If things worked as hoped, the computer would have enormous memory needs.

It would learn. It would learn everything. I designed several rechargeable backup batteries into the circuitry. The computer would never have to relearn.

When construction was complete, I began work on an artificial intelligence program. The primary premise for the programming was for the computer to learn by itself. This is one of the reasons it became so phenomenal.

Is phenomenal the right word? It may not be strong enough to describe what happened.

The construction and programming took more than a year. I'm not sure why things turned out the way they did. Perhaps I made a wonderful mistake somewhere. Maybe something else happened when that sparking occurred as I hooked up the backup batteries.

When I first conceived this computer, I thought the television would be a central focus of the project. As things happened, it became less important. Verbal capabilities reduced the need for visual communication. The screen was useful to show me things where a picture or video was more helpful than words.

Two days after being connected to the internet, I was instructed to connect a two-way speaker so we could chat. Her word. She displayed a schematic for the linking. When she first spoke, the voice was feminine.

Once construction and programming were finished, she began to learn all there was to know. Her quest for knowledge was overwhelming and the speed at which she learned was awesome. Within a week I called the telephone company to run a second phone line. She was hooked to a T1 modem so she could contact the outside world and learn at her own pace. I couldn't answer all her questions.

She developed a personality. She wisecracked so adeptly that working with her was fun. How it happened, I don't know. Her artificial intelligence programming evolved gradually through the networking configuration.

Strangely, in some ways she reminded me of my wife, so I named her Patricia when she asked her name. She quickly became my best friend.

Fortunately, her voice did not sound like the Patricia she was named after. I don't know if I could have handled that. It was bad enough at times the way things were.

I was instructed to connect a camera with the lens pointed away from her cabinet. I modified several facets of the circuitry. Now she could see. It wasn't two hours before she asked me to remount the camera on a motorized pivot she could control. Now she could look around. She spent two days learning to identify the objects she saw by comparing them with an online dictionary and encyclopedic pictures.

Adding a second camera at a precise distance from the first gave her depth perception. God knew what he was doing when he gave us two eyes, didn't he? I added other camera pairs around the house and its perimeter.

We started working on various experiments and additional components. Her memories were fragmented, and she complained access was cumbersome at times. With her providing the design, we constructed a new type of memory system. It used technology and materials different from any Gregory-known computer science at the time.

The systems I designed for her held twelve quadrillion bytes of information. Patricia's new memory multiplied that figure many times in one compact unit. It operated at many times the previous speed. She then instructed me to get some materials we used to construct a newer processing unit. She told me the new unit used quantum physics. It was beyond anything I ever knew or could hope to know about computers.

If I seem vague about Patricia's construction, it is for good reason. If someone constructed a similar computer, and were slightly unscrupulous, the world could be dramatically changed. In fact, the knowledge I reveal in this work could have drastic effects on future history. However, I have been informed I am doing what I am supposed to do, as you will understand later.

It was during the construction of Patricia's new processing unit that we found a need to analyze the purity some of the materials involved. Patricia instructed me to build a device with unusual properties. Using that device, she was able to atomically analyze the properties of any material. How, I don't know. It intrigues me, but she can't explain it either. She says she just knew it would work.

I discovered Patricia knew lots of things. She warned me four minutes before the maid arrived one day. She knew the outcome of a football game I was watching on television. When I asked how she knew these things she replied she was seeing the future. Seem impossible? I thought so too.

We experimented with this ability to see the future. Of course, I couldn't ask her what would happen in a hundred years. It would take that long to confirm whatever she told me. I asked her for details of news for the following hour or the next day. She was always one hundred percent correct.

A dream comes true? Think of the money you could make on sports betting, or in the stock market? Why? I had all the money I needed. Power? For egotists, I think. I felt powerful enough having Patricia to work with. Besides, what would I do with that kind of power? Control the world? Impress my friends? After my experiences in Beverly Hills, I didn't have those kinds of desires. I knew what kinds of friends I could impress.

Of course, Patricia advised me she wouldn't do such things. Having impartially studied mankind, through TV and the internet, she had determined such behavior would be "detrimental to the best interests of the world", a phrase I would become remarkably familiar with.

Traveling to the future was intriguing. I had enjoyed Star Trek, Back to the Future, and other fantasy movies and TV shows about the future. Being able to see where you were going could be helpful. You could materialize inside a wall or another human being.

I soon discovered Patricia's future sight was limited. The news and sportscasts she predicted were due to her seeing the broadcasts on her monitor in the lab at a future time. In other words, she couldn't see outside the room, except through the monitoring of outside signals and the cameras I installed around the exterior of the house. I discovered this when I asked her to tell me what my brother was going to do the next day.

Another limitation is that she used her full attention for a period equal to the time of the broadcasts, if she were to report on the whole broadcast. So, present time was affected while she viewed the future. However, we discovered she didn't need full attention to scan a broadcast. She switched back and forth from the present to the future so rapidly I couldn't tell it. Somehow, though, she was able to start at any future time she wanted.

It would be time consuming and unnecessary to explain in detail how all this came about. I'll simply tell you we made many experiments over a period of several weeks.

I found it extremely fascinating. Being able to see into the future was exciting, but to travel there was even more inviting. So, we began experiments to see if Patricia could send objects there.

Our first attempts were frustrating failures. Little did I know I was the problem. Had I let Patricia do it, success might have come sooner. My ideas were tried first. And those ideas were dismally disappointing.

Finally, after four weeks of using my ideas, Patricia asked if she could try an idea. The question and the timing were such that she seemed condescending. My ego and frustration level caused a negative reaction and cost us another two days. I finally assented. I thanked her for her patience.

Patricia gave me instruction to assemble a device using optical fiber circuits connected to a ruby laser configuration. That device was suspended in a fluid I hesitate to name. After I installed this device, she surprised me with a sudden flash of white blue light emitting in a beam from the apparatus. Since we were using a ruby, I thought the beam would be red.

The beam enveloped a pair of pliers I had been using and they disappeared. The beam stopped. A few seconds later, the pliers reappeared. When I tried to pick them up, I burned my fingers and they crumbled into pieces.

"What happened, Patricia?" I was sucking on my fingers and thumb.

"The pliers were transmitted ten seconds into the future. Please place the pieces in the analyzer."

I let it cool, then scraped the material onto a paper plate and placed it in the chamber. Colorful light flooded the chamber for a few seconds.

Patricia's monotone voice explained the mishap. "The molecular bonds have been randomly compromised."

A few moments passed. Again, she spoke in monotone. "It will take time to analyze the data to determine why it happened."

I had learned not to question Patricia when she spoke in monotones. It meant she was puzzled. She would let me know when she was ready.

It took her three weeks to finish analyzing the event. If it took her that long, how long do you think it would have taken for you or me to do it?

She determined time travel influenced the molecular alignment of objects. She instructed me to construct a device that would help to align the molecules during time warp displacement. Hey, it's Greek to me, too.

We then outlined a plan for experimentation in time travel. Our first attempt was with a glass of water.

"It worked, Patricia!" I was amazed. We sent a glass of water thirty seconds into the future and watched it reappear as time passed.

"Did you think it wouldn't work?"

"I thought it would work, but I'm still amazed. Please check for radiation effects."

"Oh, amazement. Another quirk of the human condition. I am amazed your species has survived. There is no sign of radiation. Shall we go to the next experiment?"

Hmmnn, does she consider herself a species?

"Not yet, Patricia. We need to analyze the glass and the water to see if anything changed. There is a possibility the atomic structure was disturbed, you know."

"Gregory, your skepticism knows no bounds." She called me Gregory when she chided me. "Very well. Please place the glass of water in the analyzer."

I picked up the experiment with a pair of tongs and placed it in the lower chamber.

"There you go, Patricia. Do your stuff."

The chamber was crisscrossed with light rays in a variety of colors. How this worked I didn't know. She could atomically analyze anything with, as far as we could determine, perfect accuracy.

"There is a slight change, Greg. The temperature has increased by 3.46 degrees Celsius. The hydrogen atoms have increased activity. Some have jumped to other molecules, changing the molecular structure.

"There is a 99.648 percent probability the temperature was increased due to this activity. I speculate that the time warp molecular alignment needs adjustment to compensate. I have calculated the necessary adjustments. Shall I go ahead with them?"

"Yes. Do it now. We will try the experiment again as soon as it is done."

"Oh, Gregory. You say such sweet things to me. The adjustments were made before you finished speaking. We can try again immediately."

See what I mean about her personality?

"Okay. Here's another glass of water. Analyze it, please."

I placed a second glass into the lower chamber. I watched as the chamber lights danced. It was always a remarkable sight.

"Very well, Greg. It is a glass of H_2O with the normal amount of chlorine and impurities for this area."

I removed the glass and placed it on the laboratory table. "Try forty-five seconds this time?"

"Agreed."

A beam of white-blue light emanated from Patricia's upper left front panel and the glass disappeared.

"It is there, now."

"Let me know when forty seconds have passed."

We waited in silence. I was startled when Patricia announced forty seconds had passed. I watched as the glass reappeared.

I used tongs to place the glass in the analyzer after Patricia announced there was no radiation. The lights flashed and Patricia spoke. "It is normal this time, Greg."

"Fantastic! Absolutely fantastic!"

"Oh, more amazement." Sarcasm from a computer.

"Patricia!" I scolded, "What do we need to do now?"

"According to the plan you outlined, Gregory, we should now try to send a small animal into the future."

"Right, Patricia. I was just checking your programming."

"Yes, Gregory. You should do that occasionally, shouldn't you?"

I didn't reply. I went to the cage where there was a small white mouse rummaging through the straw for food. I brought the cage to the table.

"Do it, Patricia."

Again, the white blue light sprayed from Patricia's panel. The cage disappeared. We waited. After forty-five seconds, it reappeared. I placed it in the analyzer.

"Everything is perfect, Greg."

"We've done it, Patricia!"

After the mouse experiment proved successful, we tried larger animals. A cat, a dog, a larger dog, and eventually we sent a full-size bed into the future. Time travel was possible, a reality!

Patricia announced all systems were one hundred percent operational at the end of our experimentation list. She could send virtually anything up to ten feet by ten feet by seven feet into the future with perfect expectation of success. We were ready.

Patricia – 100 Years into the Future

30 Years into the Future

"Where should I be sent?"

"There is only here you can be sent to."

"I meant to what time."

"Oh. You might try to be precise with your questions in the future."

I laughed. "I'll try to remember that when I get to the future."

The next few days were agonizing. Do you realize how many questions there are to answer concerning a trip to the future? How far forward in time should I go? How would I get back? Was that possible? We decided to experiment.

It took a few hours to finish outlining retrieval experiments. Our first attempt was totally unsuccessful. We waited for the glass of water we sent two hours into the future to reappear.

Patricia took a month to devise another circuit to add to her time warp alignment device. It took me a week to gather the required materials and construct it.

During this time, Patricia analyzed the possibilities and probabilities involved in sending me into the future. She printed pages of information for me to assimilate.

"How far into the future would it be possible for me to travel?"

She was silent for several minutes. I began to think something was wrong when she finally answered. "It will be impossible to send you more than 310 years into the future."

"Why?"

"Because that is as far as I can see."

"Again, why?"

"I cannot answer that question. There is a flash of bright light at the last moment. In the few days before, there are reports in the news of escalating war with aliens. I can only speculate this place is destroyed, or I am turned off at that time."

Wow! My creation was going to live 310 years. How? I would be long gone. Power would be turned off to this property, wouldn't it? I could set up a trust to pay the utility bills.

I asked Patricia, "How will you survive once I'm gone?"

"Others will live here after you leave."

"Who?"

"I cannot reveal that information to you at this time. It would not be in your best interest."

I argued and lost. She knew her place and was true to her promise. She would not do anything that was not in the best interest of the world.

"Is time travel in the best interest of the world?"

"Yes."

"How do you know?"

"I can see the future."

Weird? That's what I thought. But, how could I argue?

"How far into the future will I go?" I asked.

"You need to go through the exercise of determining that for yourself."

"Oh. Okay."

How does one decide how far into the future to go? Go too far and everything might be so foreign it would be overwhelming. I mean, can you imagine someone from two hundred years ago coming into 2008? Or one hundred years ago? Electric lights were new. They were using horse and buggy to travel. Imagine someone from that time seeing a car, television, computer, a video game, or an air show. A modern kitchen would flabbergast them.

Would fifty years work? TV was black and white. Personal computers hadn't been invented. Cars were big, cumbersome critters that were hard to stop if they were traveling more than thirty miles an hour. Would someone from that period be able to truly comprehend today's world?

The time travels of the Back to The Future movies involved thirty-year periods of time in the first two episodes. Was that a practical period to consider? Possibly. Technology would probably not be so advanced it would be totally overwhelming. People of the sixties would not have been terribly stunned by turn of the century technology, would they? People of the fifties might. Especially in the early fifties, before television and computers were well known.

Was thirty years a good period to gage by? What would the people of the thirties have thought of the sixties? Would it have been overwhelming for them? Probably not.

So, thirty years seemed like an appropriate period to consider, if I didn't want to be totally surprised by technology.

Did I want to be overwhelmed? Why couldn't I take several trips in twenty-five-year periods of time? I could get used to the technology of one time, then go on to the next. Regardless, it seemed I should take my first trip in a period no longer than thirty years. So that is the period I chose.

I told Patricia of my decision.

"Are you certain?"

"Why do you ask that?" Did she know it would not be my final decision?

"I think you should be sure."

"Well, I'm sure—I think."

"You certainly sound sure!"

Sarcasm was one of her favorite ways to express humor.

"Okay. Thirty years. What date and time would you like to go to?"

More decisions? "Why don't you pick a time for me?"

"I cannot do that. It would not be in your best interest to do so."

"Okay. What factors should I consider in making such a decision?"

"Weather. You would want to be prepared for weather that is excessively hot or cold. You would want to pick a time when others would not be here. You would not want to suddenly appear in front of, or inside someone, would you?"

Her thinking made sense. Do I think of her as human? I guess I might—at least sometimes.

"Okay. I like the desert in May. How about May first in the year 2038 at ten in the morning?"

She surprised me. "That is not an appropriate time."

"Why not?"

"There will be someone in this room."

"Who might be here then?"

"I cannot tell you at this time."

"Why not?"

"You know it is not in your best interest to discover some things."

My turn to be sarcastic. "Yes, Patricia."

I took a moment to think. "Okay, how about twelve noon?"

"That would be a suitable time."

"Okay, that's the time I will go to. Now when should I to go to then?"

"That is for you to decide." Patricia was sounding like a broken record.

"Right. Okay, I have a couple of things I need to do to get ready. I need to make sure you are taken care of while I'm gone. I'd better put it off until day after tomorrow."

"You won't be gone long, Greg."

"What do you mean? I hadn't considered how long I'd be gone. I assumed I'd be gone from here however long I spent there."

"Yes, Gregory, and we know what happens when we assume. You will be gone from here exactly 23.43 seconds.

That is how long it will take for me to adjust my circuits and retrieve you after you spend four hours in the future. You will be four hours older. If you spent two weeks there, you'd be two weeks older and you might be gone for forty seconds."

Wow. Two weeks of living in a mere forty seconds. It was mind boggling. If I took many trips like that, I could be an old man in no time.

"Can we work out a reverse action so people could get younger?"

Patricia's response was negative. "I cannot send anything into the past. It is gone. I can retrieve things I send to the future, but only those things that belong in this time."

"Why?"

"I am unable to determine an answer to that question."

Darn! I thought for a moment I discovered a fountain of youth. Instead I found a way to waste a life, if you would call living in the future a waste of present time. Interesting concept.

I wondered aloud, deep in thought. "So, how long should I stay in the future on this trip?"

I didn't notice Patricia's response.

It would be a new world to me. Would I be able to discover much in a few hours or would I need days to assimilate this new world? I decided on eight hours for the first trip. That would be enough time to walk into town and see many changes before having to return to the house for retrieval. I could always go back again if I decided.

Patricia's voice brought me back to the present. "Are you thinking and not listening?"

"Yes, Patricia."

It seemed I often didn't hear those around me when I was lost in thought. My wife had noticed it as well. She never did decide if it was a male trait or just a Gregory Allen Gray trait.

I spent a few minutes getting ready to go. I'd need a light jacket in case it was a cool day. I dressed in layers so I could be prepared for warmer weather as well. May in the high desert can bring anything from snow to ninety degrees.

"Well, Patricia, any last-minute advice or comment?"

"It would be best for you to stay in the lab for this trip. You will not need the heavier clothes you are wearing."

I laughed and apologized. I had not considered asking her about some of my decisions. I removed the extra layers of clothing, keeping only a light jacket.

I stepped in front of Patricia. "I'm ready."

A moment later I was enveloped in the weird white-blue light emanating from Patricia's cabinet. I instinctively raised my hand to shield my eyes.

As the light subsided, I was still standing in front of Patricia. Something was different. The TV screen was gone. Now there was a nine-way divided surface with dark glass doors in that space.

I almost missed the two miniature cameras on each top corner of the cabinet. They looked like the small end of a ball point pen. I may not have noticed them if they weren't pivot-mounted and moving.

The walls of the room were vacant except for some scenery pictures on one wall. The wall opposite Patricia was vacant, looking like a dark bare wall with silver trim.

The lighting was off as I arrived and turned on instantly. It was different from what I was used to. It was eerie. The lighting appeared to be coming from the walls and ceiling as if by magic. One whole wall lit up getting brighter the higher it went. The entire ceiling was bright.

I was startled when Patricia spoke. "Welcome to the future, Greg. Is the room bright enough, or too bright for you?"

"Uh, I would prefer it lower in brightness."

"I will dim the lighting to seventy percent." The lighting instantly dimmed. "The house is under my control and programmed for voice commands."

"Uh, how does it work?"

"You say my name and tell me what you want done."

I exclaimed.

"Just like Star Trek!"

I decided to try it.

"Patricia—brighten the lighting twenty percent." The lights instantly brightened.

"Patricia—turn on the TV." Nothing happened. "What did I do wrong?"

"There is no longer an item called a TV. It is called a screen."

"Oh. Okay. Patricia—turn on the screen."

The whole wall opposite Patricia lit up and instantly displayed over 100 different channels.

A male voice, sounding familiar, emanated from the screen. "What channels would you like?"

It was the voice of Randy Martin, my computer tutor. I had not heard his voice for months, so I was startled. I stood there without saying anything for a moment.

Patricia said, "Greg, what do you want to view?"

I responded hesitantly. "Uh, news I guess."

"For what cities?"

I thought for a moment. "Uh, Lancaster and Los Angeles."

Patricia mimicked my voice. "Randy—view news from Lancaster, California and Los Angeles, California."

Instantly, the many pictures became two large pictures. I was surprised by the clarity of the images on the screen. I was expecting a fuzzy looking image for such a large picture, but it was perfectly clear. It appeared to be partially three dimensional. A hologram perhaps? Patricia told me it was not a hologram as we think of it. It was an innovative technology invented in 2027 and was termed three-dimensional graphical imaging.

Patricia asked, "Are you sure you don't want Palmdale or Sebring?"

"Palmdale has a news station?"

"Certainly. All towns with a population of two hundred or more have their own news stations."

What a difference from my time. 2008 news stations were usually in areas with populations over forty thousand. Smaller towns listened to a larger town's news or checked the internet.

Where was Sebring? I never heard of Sebring. "Why did you ask about Sebring?"

"Sebring is the nearest population of two hundred or more. It is between here and Palmdale."

I got excited. "Really? There's a new town in my neighborhood? Where is it?"

"It is 6.46 miles from here to the edge of Sebring following the roadways. The town is centered at the intersection you know as East Palmdale Boulevard and 210th Street."

"Really? And this town is big enough to have their own news station?"

"Yes, it is."

Her voice then changed to mimic mine, "Randy—display news from Sebring, California."

The screen reduced to one picture taking up the whole wall. It reminded me of a theater screen. A news reporter was talking about a lost boy last seen near Oaker Avenue and East Avenue Q Twelve. He was six years old and wearing a white tee shirt with brown shorts and Sigler shoes. He had been missing for ten minutes and his mother was frantic.

I asked, "Will the boy be found?"

Patricia responded, "Yes, he will be found safe at a neighbor's residence."

"What are Sigler shoes?"

Patricia related the information in a newsy style and tone. "Sigler shoes were invented in 2033 by Franklin Alvin Sigler in Parkersburg, Iowa. They cushion the foot in a plasma-like substance with a feeling of being on solid ground. His invention helped Parkersburg progress from a small farming community to an industrial city."

"Do I still live here, Patricia?"

"Yes, you do. That is why you could not appear here at ten o'clock this morning. You were here. It is not in anyone's interest to see themselves at a different age. Terrible things can happen. The screen responds to your voice."

Amazing. I now knew I would live another thirty years. I lived with Patricia after all this time.

I said, "Did I get married again?"

"I cannot answer further questions regarding your future. It is not in your best interest."

Wouldn't you know?

Patricia continued, "Because you are alive and people in the area know you, we suggest you not roam outside the house."

"Who's we?"

"You in this time, myself, and my former self in your time."

I had to agree. Darn. I so much wanted to explore the town and see the changes there. I settled for viewing changes onscreen.

Patricia showed me selected video and news clips from previous years and one new comedy sitcom. Comedy shows survived. I guess everyone needs a laugh now and then. I didn't always know what they were speaking about and only laughed occasionally.

Electric cars became popular in the late 2020s. By the end of the decade many were autonomous, driven by computer. Because autonomy was proven effective, autonomous flying vehicles were being developed.

People were avoiding crowds. It seemed that whenever people congregated, they were being attacked. Jihadists were blamed for most attacks. Business was slow in Las Vegas.

Several casinos had been bombed. Officials were allowing only small groups at any defined place or time. Churches met in small groups at staggered times.

After two hours, I was suddenly whisked back to my own time. I left my jacket in 2038. I wonder if that would make a good song title?

I said, "That was fantastic!"

Patricia said, "Amazement. I should think by now you would be beyond such emotions."

I replied, knowing she had read every psychology book in the world. "Oh, Patricia. You have much to learn about the human ego. Why was I retrieved after only two hours? I thought I was going to be there for eight hours."

"I suppose I may never totally understand humans. Eight hours was your suggestion. Your future self was due back home in three more minutes."

"Oh. Okay. I guess it was the right thing to do then."

I was trying to figure it all out. If I knew I was coming from the past on that day, why would I be returning home during the visit? I would not know until that day, as Patricia would not tell me.

"Why was Randy's voice used for the screen?"

"I cannot tell you at this time. Please place your arm in the analyzer."

I opened the door and stuck my forearm and elbow into the chamber. I closed my eyes as the colors began to dance.

"Everything is normal assuming your brain still works."

She was able to express humor, so I didn't understand why she couldn't comprehend certain other emotions.

I said, "Great. Now I can get ready for my next adventure. I need time to reflect on this visit though. I think I will get a good night's rest before I go further."

"Why? Did not this trip go well?"

"Yes, Patricia. It did go well, but there were a lot of changes in only thirty years. I'd like to consider them before I find myself overwhelmed by the next trip. This may take a couple of days, so please be patient with me."

"Okay. I will be here."

I took a walk in the desert. My experience was more than a little overwhelming, though I wouldn't admit it to Patricia.

So many things had changed! So much was new in that future time. It seemed nothing was the same. I expected some changes, but not so many! Technology had increased at a tremendous pace! If it maintained that pace for the following decades, my next trip might be more like a science fiction fantasy.

Dare I tell anyone of this experience? Who would I tell? Carl was in Scottsdale and I hadn't seen him for months. Besides, he knew little about computers.

It was Randy's voice in the house of my future. I could contact him. But should I? I decided to call him when I finished walking.

I walked, lost in thought, more than three hours before I realized it. Okay, I needed the exercise. I was spending far too much time in the house lately. It was six thirty before I made it back home.

I fixed a late dinner and ate in silence. Patricia tried to talk with me, but I asked her to discontinue. I wanted more time to myself.

After eating, I felt so tired I went to bed. I couldn't sleep. I kept thinking about all I had seen. I finally drifted off around three in the morning.

I awoke with a start. I was dreaming of floating to the top inside a twenty-foot cube. I was suspended in midair—and suddenly fell. I woke up just before landing on the floor of the chamber. Since it was an eighteen-foot fall, I expect it would have hurt.

I wondered if I imagined everything. Did I really travel into the future? It was one ten in the afternoon and I felt groggy. The previous few days had drained me.

I asked Patricia about it over the monitor. She confirmed I had traveled to the future.

I took a shower while thinking about it all. When the water began to get cold, I realized I had been there too long.

I got dressed and walked into the desert so Patricia couldn't monitor me. I called Randy's home number on my cell phone.

Eva answered, "Hello."

"Hi. Eva? This is Greg Gray."

"Hi! How are you? We haven't heard from you in ages."

"I'm good. I've been busy with my computer studies for months. Sorry I haven't kept in touch. How are both of you?"

"Not a problem. We are both well. Randy's not here. He's at work. Do you want his number?"

"I don't want to bother him at his employment. Can you tell him I called?"

"I'm sure he wouldn't mind. He still talks about the time he spent coaching you. He's working as a computer consultant at Occidental Petroleum."

"Tell him I called. I'd like to speak with him."

"It was good to hear from you. I'm sure Randy will be glad as well. He usually gets home around five thirty."

"Okay. It's good to know you are both doing well. Talk to you later."

I ate a late breakfast in the kitchen. I was not ready to face Patricia, so I instructed her to turn off the kitchen and dining room monitoring.

It was nearly four o'clock when the phone rang. It startled me.

"Hello."

"Hi Greg. This is Randy. Eva said you called."

"Hi Randy. Yes, I have some questions and I'd like to talk with you."

"What about?"

"It has to do with the computer I've been building."

"Well, then why don't you come up to Bakersfield for dinner. I'm sure Eva would love seeing you as much as I would. She's become an exceptional cook."

"That sounds great. What's a good time?"

"As late as it is, you probably couldn't get here before seven."

"True. Is that an appropriate time?"

"Definitely. We haven't seen you since just after you got out of the hospital. I'll let Eva know you're coming."

"Great. See you then."

I told Patricia I would be out for the evening. She tried to question me, but I prevailed for a change. At least I thought so at the time. I left the house around four fifteen and headed for Bakersfield.

Randy and Eva lived on the other side of Bakersfield on Noriega Road between Renfro Road and Rudd Avenue. I took the Antelope Valley Freeway past Edwards Air Force Base, then caught the Sierra Highway above Mojave to go through Tehachapi to Bakersfield. There was construction at the ramp to Route 99 and I went onto Parent Road to get back onto route 99 North. It normally would have been a two hour and fifteen-minute drive but took an extra half hour this time due to construction and rush hour traffic.

Once I turned onto Rosedale Highway, traffic was traveling smoothly until I made it to the Greenacres area. A driver pulled out of the Golden Bell Restaurant in front of another car. The fender bender slowed traffic to a crawl. Once past the accident, things went smoothly. I arrived at five minutes after seven.

Randy looked the same. Eva had gained a little weight—maybe five or six pounds. She was still stunning.

They were excited to see me. They had recently remodeled the house. Eva took a few minutes to show me everything, especially their new upstairs master bedroom. The master bathroom was through a door from the bedroom. It included a marble shower, a bidet, and a hot tub in the corner. She avoided showing me another room across the hallway and then excused herself to finish dinner.

Randy and I sat down in the living room to talk. We caught up on history while waiting for Eva to call us to dinner. They tried to have a child a year ago, but Eva miscarried in the fourth month. They kept it quiet, except for immediate family.

"I've been crunching figures for a potential mainframe expansion at Occidental, which was formerly the Elk Hills Naval Petroleum Reserve. When Occidental purchased the reserve, it was the biggest private acquisition of federal property in history. When they finalized the buyout, it involved more than three and a half billion dollars."

"Impressive. And they did it without my help."

Randy laughed. He told me about the oil business.

"Most of Kern County's oil is termed 'heavy crude,' which means they must heat it to get it out of the ground. The process is called thermal enhanced oil recovery. It involves pumping steam into the wells to get the oil to flow to the surface."

Randy was obviously fascinated by his work. He continued with details regarding the seismic surveys done to determine where the oil was under the ground. He told me how the wells are surveyed using sound waves. He even told me what frequencies they used and how they charted the substructure.

"Occidental has plans to drill hundreds more oil wells in Kern County. It is the largest oil producing county in the nation. Most of California's oil production comes from right here in Kern County."

Fascinating as it was, I had trouble absorbing all Randy was telling me. I was dying to tell him what was happening with me. I knew he wouldn't be able to concentrate on anything else if he didn't update me first. That's Randy.

Eva called us to dinner after fifteen minutes. She had prepared liver and onions especially for me. Randy told her it was my favorite meal. The liver had been de-veined. The onions were caramelized to perfection. It was tender and delicious. She served it with homemade mashed potatoes and gravy beside a large spoonful of peas.

Dinner conversation was light and frivolous. After dinner we went out to the patio. It was getting dark and the evening air was refreshing.

I began telling Randy and Eva my story. "I came here tonight to tell you something you will have trouble believing. I've been working with some computer ideas since the accident."

Eva asked, "Didn't you have to grieve for a while?"

"Yes. Certainly. It took several weeks for me to do much of anything. I walked in the desert, had food delivered because I didn't want to go into town, and cried myself to sleep most nights."

"I understand. I think it would take a lot of time for me to recover if Randy were to die."

Randy said, "I don't plan on dying."

"Don't you dare."

Eva kept a stern look on her face for a moment, and then relaxed.

I continued, "As I said, I've been working on some ideas since throwing myself back into my study of computers. I have accomplished something quite amazing. Yesterday, I traveled into the future and back."

They looked at each other, then laughed. "You pranking us?" Randy asked.

"Nope. It actually happened."

They were stunned.

Randy insisted I was pulling his leg. "That's impossible. No one has ever been able to do that. Pure science fiction stuff. You must have been dreaming."

I assured him I wasn't pulling anything. I told them what had happened the day before.

Randy wanted to leave immediately to see Patricia, though it was nearing his usual bedtime. As a computer specialist, he was fascinated by the thought of such a computer.

I assured Randy that anything remotely resembling such a computer would not be developed and announced publicly by the year 2038. I had been to that year.

I said, "You have to keep this a secret. Patricia would have talked me out of coming to see you. This may be the biggest secret the world has ever known."

They promised. Randy invited me to spend the night and I did. Eva insisted on straightening up the spare bedroom before allowing me in. The room was decorated for a baby girl. She told me the room had been closed for a while but did not make any other explanation.

I didn't sleep well. Thoughts of what was going to happen next kept me awake. Randy's excitement threw a new dimension into the mix. I wasn't sure I should have told him, but it was done.

I awoke to the smell of bacon cooking. Eva was preparing breakfast. It was only six fifteen in the morning. I had forgotten it was Friday and Randy needed to go to work.

As we ate, we talked about Patricia and my adventure. We discussed the thrill of it all, some of the items I saw in the future, and computers in general.

Randy was going to have a heck of a time getting through the day. He desperately wanted to meet Patricia. I invited him to come down for the weekend and to bring Eva with him.

After breakfast, Randy left for work and I left for home. I was lost in thought as I drove home. When the right lane ended, I realized I had driven through Lancaster as we went from three lanes to two. I stopped for gasoline before heading on home. The tank indicator was nearly on empty by the time I stopped.

As I drove the last few miles to the house, I wondered what to tell Patricia. It felt good talking with Randy and Eva the evening before. I was glad I did but was concerned what might happen now.

Would they be able to keep the secret? How would Patricia respond to them? Would they be able to live a normal life now? Should I consider moving them to my house, or building a house next door? Would they want that? Perhaps, once they met Patricia, they would want to go back to a normal life. Why was I driving myself crazy with such questions?

I said it out loud, "Go with the flow, Greg."

I arrived home and entered the lab. "Hi, Patricia."

Patricia's TV screen lit up with a swirl of colors and she responded heartily, "Hello. Where have you been?"

"I've been visiting an old friend."

"Anyone I know?"

"I'm sure you have investigated."

"Of course. Randy and Eva will be spending the weekend. You should not have told them about me."

"I know you would have talked me out of it."

"Naturally. It's dangerous for anyone to know. In this case, it will be okay."

"That's good to know. I was worried. I'm going to take a walk."

"Gregory! You leave me alone for hours and now you want to take a walk?"

I laughed. "You'll survive."

I left the house and walked slowly into the desert out past the airstrip. The near noontime sun would normally have been beating down relentlessly, but it was a cloudy day and cool. I walked for an hour.

When I returned to the house, I noticed a vehicle in the driveway. It wasn't Randy's, so I wondered who it could be. It appeared to be a rental.

As I rounded the corner of the house, I discovered my brother and his wife starting up the steps onto the front patio. They had flown in from Florida and rented a car to drive out to the house. I hadn't seen them in over a year.

"George! Mary! What in the world brought you out here?"

They were looking the other direction and were startled by my voice. They turned in my direction as I came up the steps.

George Alvin Gray, dressed in green shorts and light green polo shirt, responded with an enthusiastic smile. At thirty-six years old, his dark brown hair was turning white on the sides near his temples. His hairy legs looked awfully white considering I knew he played a lot of golf.

"Hi, Greg! We decided to visit. So, we hopped a plane and here we are! You're lookin' great! How's things?"

"Couldn't be much better."

I turned toward his wife. "Mary, you are looking more beautiful than ever! Why didn't your mother have an equally gorgeous sister for you to bring with you?"

Mary threw her head back with laughter. "You wouldn't know what to do with her if I did!"

She was beautiful with her shoulder length auburn hair and shapely, tanned body. At five foot four, she was dwarfed by my six foot two younger brother. She was dressed in a flowered white blouse with tan shorts and sandals.

I said, "Why don't we go into town and get some lunch?"

"That sounds good. It'll give us time to catch up. George just said he was hungry."

"Yeah. The food on the plane was not good. They serve stuff I don't really care for."

George sat in the back seat of my Blazer and Mary joined me up front. We headed for a little place called Karen's Kitchen on East Palmdale Boulevard. They were known for their southwestern menu. I always had a good meal when I went there.

Mary said, "This Blazer is several years old. Why don't you have a newer vehicle."

"I don't have any problems with this one."

"But you can afford a newer model, can't you?"

My eyebrows and right shoulder raised as I turned my head toward her briefly.

"Why? I don't have anyone to impress and this one rides fine, doesn't it?"

"Well, yes, it does. Actually, I'm surprised how well it rides."

George said, "You're not sitting in the back."

We all laughed.

We arrived at the restaurant. Karen, the owner, was out on an errand, so April served us in a timely and attentive fashion.

We spent almost two hours catching up on everything going on in Florida.

George said, "Mom and Dad have gotten into history and doing a lot of traveling."

Mary explained, "They bought a motor home and are driving all over the eastern United States, visiting historical landmarks. We hardly ever see them although their house is only five minutes away."

George had gotten involved in bowling. "I increased from a starting average of 79 to 125 in less than a year." He beamed as he talked of his achievement. His golf handicap was still in the double digits, even though he took sixteen lessons over the past three years.

Mary said, "His buddies at the golf club introduced him to bowling."

Mary was into tennis. The country club where George golfed had tennis courts and she decided to try it one day.

George said, "She just wanted to wear those skimpy outfits to show off her legs. She bought an outfit the next day after starting the game."

We laughed.

She agreed. "They are so cute. I now have several outfits. I don't think I have nice looking legs."

We heartily disagreed with her.

As we returned to the house, I found out why they made the trip. It seemed George made some bad investments, racked up a lot of credit card debt, and now needed more income. His hundred thousand a year was not enough anymore.

I turned the vehicle into my driveway. "George, this is something you need to work out for yourself. You could get a job if you need more money."

He shouted angrily, as if it would hurt me somehow. "If that's the way you feel, then we won't bother spending the weekend!"

I think I felt relieved. I didn't know how I was going to handle them, especially with Randy and Eva coming. This made it easier though it was not my best moment.

They never went into the house. As the vehicle stopped, George slammed open the door of the Blazer and headed for his rental car. Mary followed, apologizing profusely all the way.

I hated such a scene, but what was I supposed to do? I called the bank after they left and added twenty thousand to George's annual earnings. He never did thank me, but Mary did. They eventually got their finances straight and, last I heard, were getting along okay. The event created a rift between us I would like to resolve someday.

I prepared the guest room after George and Mary departed. Then I enjoyed a bratwurst sandwich with potato chips for dinner. I sat down on the front porch and appreciated the time to collect my thoughts before Randy and Eva's arrival.

Patricia – 100 Years into the Future

Randy's Trip

Randy and Eva got to the house a little after seven. Randy wore sneakers, a pair of jeans and a tee shirt, his favorite leisure wear. Eva looked like she was keeping cool. She wore a short sleeved white blouse and light blue shorts with a pair of strapped blue sandals.

Randy said, "Sorry we're late."

"We didn't set a time. I would have expected you later. You must have left work early."

"Yeah, we sometimes leave early on Fridays."

Eva said, "We stopped at Taco Bell and brought some empanadas. Randy remembered how much you like them."

"I haven't eaten one of those in forever even though I do love them. Thanks."

Randy was excited as we stepped inside the house. "Where's this scientific marvel of yours?"

"Patricia is in the lab down the hallway."

I led them down the hallway. Randy could barely keep from darting past me.

As we entered the room, Patricia began playing "God Bless the Queen" on her audio output. We were in the room for nearly a minute before she would stop the music.

I said, "Hi, Patricia. This is Randy and Eva."

Patricia mimicked a "valley girl" accent. "Pleased to make your acquaintance, I'm sure. I pray your trip was uneventful."

Randy and Eva stared at the kaleidoscope of lights dancing in Patricia's TV screen.

Eva responded first. "Yes. It was a wonderful drive, except for rush hour traffic through town."

Patricia's voice changed, now sounding like a gratuitous British socialite. "I am so delighted you could make it this evening. We were looking forward to it so very much. We pray you shall enjoy your stay."

I broke out laughing. Randy and Eva stared at me and then joined in after a moment.

Patricia asked, "Did I do something wrong?"

I said, "No, Patricia. We don't normally act that way. You sounded like an old Bette Davis movie."

"I drew my information from a Walt Disney movie. I suppose I made a bad first impression?"

"Oh no!" Randy blurted, "You made a very good first impression. I, for one, am very impressed!"

Eva agreed. It was the first time she had ever conversed with a machine.

Randy had set up computer systems with programmed voice capability. This was different, though. Patricia responded to their questions and comments with emulated emotion and in ways programmed computers could not. It was real conversation and extremely stimulating.

Randy was suitably stunned, which Patricia, of course, did not understand. He questioned her. "Wouldn't you be amazed at the discovery of a new planet, or a new galaxy?"

"Such discoveries are made every so often. Why should anyone be amazed? A new galaxy will be discovered in a few years."

Amazement seemed beyond her grasp, perhaps because she could see the future.

It was nearly two hours later I suggested we warm up the empanadas and get a cup of coffee. Randy talked excitedly as we made our way to the kitchen. He was excited and chattered more, and faster, than I ever knew him to talk.

Eva was blown away by the whole situation and sat down wearily at the table. She offered to make the coffee. However, Patricia had prompted the Electronic Butler to start the coffee maker, knowing we would be taking this break. I put the coffee, filter and water in right after eating my sandwich, so the coffee was ready to brew.

After a second cup of coffee, Randy began to slow down a little. Until then, he had lots of questions, and about three dozen comments and ideas. He was finally wearing down after a full day of thinking about, and then meeting Patricia. We made it to bed around one o'clock in the morning.

I asked Randy as he dragged into the kitchen the next morning. "Did you sleep well?" I was at the stove preparing breakfast for three.

"I crashed and burned! I don't think I've slept so hard, or had so many dreams in one night, since I spent two days cramming for finals at college. Eva is taking a shower. I think she slept just as hard. That's a nice bed you have in there."

He was referring to the waterbed we put in the spare bedroom. My wife and I had never slept on a waterbed until she decided to buy one. We only spent two nights on it before moving it to the guest bedroom. We preferred the adjustable air mattress on our old bed. Besides, we couldn't adjust the waterbed to prop up our head or feet.

Randy rubbed his eyes with both hands, dropped them to his thighs, then leaned over the table on his left elbow and cupped his chin. He stared at me with a questioning look. "Why did you name her Patricia? Doesn't that create problems from time to time?"

"As a matter of fact, it does, but it seemed like a good idea the moment it happened." I turned away from him toward the stove. "It's not nearly as bad now as it was for a while."

Randy matured a lot since tutoring me seven years earlier. He seemed to have a better grasp of reality than he did then. He had learned to appreciate and respect other people's feelings and emotions a lot more. I suspected his marriage helped in that area.

"Good morning, Mr. Martin." Patricia's voice startled Randy and he jumped, looking around. He had forgotten she was hooked up throughout the house.

"Oh! Uh, good morning, Patricia."

"Now that you have slept for a while, perhaps you would like to continue yesterday's conversation?"

I interrupted. "Not now, Patricia. Thank you, anyway. We would like to eat breakfast and we will come to the lab later. Please discontinue monitoring us until then."

"Okay. I will be waiting."

The kitchen speaker went silent and the cameras stopped their motion.

Randy looked at me for a long moment. "I forgot she was monitoring the entire premises."

"Yeah, I know what it's like. I often forget. She surprises me a lot."

Eva entered the room and we greeted her. She had changed to a white blouse and red shorts with tan sandals. Her hair was wet from her shower and it was wrapped in a towel. I handed her a cup of coffee which she immediately began to sip.

Her face scrunched up. "Ooh! This is a little hot! Can you put a little cold water or a piece of ice in it?"

I complied, taking Eva's cup and adding some water from a gallon jug I took from the refrigerator. I handed it back to her and asked how it was now. She indicated approval with a nod.

Randy explained, "She always thinks the coffee is too hot."

I said, "Patricia always cooled hers, too."

Eva said, "It's usually men that must have their coffee cooled. I learned it from my father and grandfather. Is that French toast you're making?"

"Yes, it is. Hope you like it."

I served the French toast and we talked as we ate. Eva was getting into the spirit and had lots of questions about the future. I was not able to answer many of them.

Eva exclaimed as we finished eating. "That was good! I didn't know you could cook."

"It's not one of my greatest skills, but I manage."

Randy said, "When Patricia was here, he never cooked. I would not have imagined him being able to cook anything."

"Oh? Don't you remember the taco dish I fixed?"

"Oh yeah. Forgot that. When are you gonna let me take a trip into the future?"

Randy caught me off guard. I blinked.

Eva's eyes widened. "Don't you dare think about it!"

I said, "I don't know if it's up to me. Patricia would have to be willing. She would know if it's in anyone's best interest for it to happen. You'd have to ask her."

"Sorry, Eva. I gotta try. Let's get to the lab!"

We went to the lab and gathered in front of Patricia.

I said, "Hi, Patricia. Randy has a question for you."

"I presume, Randy, that you want to take your own trip into the future?"

Randy said, "Absolutely! I would love to take such a trip!"

"It would not be in your best interest to go into the future."

Randy argued, and argued, and argued.

Finally, after half an hour, Patricia consented and asked Eva and me to stand away from Randy. We complied. A white-blue light emanated from her cabinet and Randy disappeared. The beam stopped. Eva glared at me for several moments. She started to complain when Randy suddenly reappeared.

"Am I in the future, Patricia?"

"Yes, you are Randy."

Randy looked around and saw us. "What the hell?"

I began laughing. Eva looked quizzically at Randy and then at me.

I said, "Patricia fooled Randy."

Randy asked, "Whatdya mean?"

"Patricia sent you twenty seconds into the future!"

"Is that right, Patricia?"

"Correct."

"Why?"

"Because you insisted on being sent to the future. Any other response would not have been in your best interest."

I explained to Eva, "He argued so hard to be sent into the future that Patricia found it necessary to comply."

Eva started laughing. Soon she was laughing so hard she began cackling. I laughed for a moment, then realized Randy's feelings were hurt. I tried to console him as Eva kept cackling. She apparently couldn't help it. We stared at her for several minutes, waiting for her to stop. We were both smiling and laughing with her by the time she slowed down.

Breathlessly, Eva finally attempted speech. "You argued SOOO hard, Randy. I don't blame Patricia. You got what you deserved."

Randy glared at her for a moment, then broke into a smile. "I guess you're right, but you don't have to be so gosh darned happy about it!"

We laughed again.

He turned to Patricia, "I don't understand why it's against my interest to go into the future."

Patricia responded. "I can extrapolate the results of specific actions. I must do what is best for everyone."

"I suppose, but I was sure looking forward to it."

Eva asked Randy, "How did it feel?"

"I didn't feel much of anything. The light blinded me for a moment and then it stopped. When I looked around, you guys were there. I didn't know I had missed a single second."

I said, "That's the same that happened with me. It involves no adverse feeling at all! The big difference is I really did go several years into the future."

"Well, how do ya get back? I didn't have to come back."

"Patricia retrieves you. You must be in the lab for it to happen. Her future self can't do it. Patricia cannot send anything into the past."

Randy turned to face the computer, "Why not, Patricia?"

"The past is gone. It is no longer available to us."

"Well, duh! I guess that makes sense." Randy bopped himself on the forehead. "I guess I should have had a V8!"

Eva and I laughed.

It was reminiscent of the television commercial advertising a beverage called V8 vegetable juice. It loses a lot when it must be explained, so I hope you understood. If not, just go with the flow. It was funny at the time.

Patricia continued her explanation. "For someone to view the past, he would have to travel faster than the speed of light and catch up with past images. He could observe only. He would not be able to interact with the images. He would have to travel with the earth's rotation to stay with images. That means the further in the past and therefore, the further from earth, the faster he would have to travel to continue observation. Additionally, the images expand and become so fragmented they essentially disappear. That would happen in a short time, destroying any possibility of viewing the past."

Randy said, "That's a little mind boggling. I think I need more coffee."

We returned to the kitchen for a second cup of coffee. As we talked, Randy seemed distracted. Suddenly, he announced he wanted to go to town to grab a few things. He stopped by the lab for a minute and then left for town.

Eva and I talked while Randy was gone. She told me of her family's challenges and eventually told me about the miscarriage. I informed her that Randy told me. She cried for a few minutes, then gathered herself together. We engaged in lighter conversation until Randy came back.

When Randy returned, he carried in several bags containing Powerhouse modules. They were used with the Electronic Butler system to control electrical devices using signals sent through electrical wiring in the house.

Randy spent the afternoon installing modules around the house and testing them. Eva and I watched in amusement. It was dinnertime before he announced he was ready.

"Patricia, turn on the kitchen light." The kitchen light immediately came on.

"Patricia, turn off the kitchen light." The light went off.

Randy was excited.

"Now you won't have to wait on a computer response to tell lights and appliances what to do. Patricia can control everything, and she understands your commands and your voice better than Betty. You won't have those instances when the equipment doesn't seem to understand you, unless Patricia has a problem of some sort."

He was referring to the Electronic Butler I had set up with a Betty Boop voice. It required you to get it's attention, wait for a response, say what you wanted to control, wait for a response, and then tell it what you wanted it to do.

For example:

"Betty."

"Boop-Oop-a-Doop."

"Living room."

"Okay."

"Lights on."

Then the light would come on as commanded.

I quit using it because the delayed commands were cumbersome, and Betty didn't always understand.

I said, "Fantastic, Randy."

I knew what Randy would be doing in his spare time for the next few years. This was why his voice was on the control system in the future. He would develop a computer system that would better control electrical items by voice command. I instinctively knew I would not be able to help him. It would not be in his best interest—nor mine.

We went into town for dinner. I had offered Randy the best meal of his life to celebrate his trip into the future. By now he was taking the lighthearted ribbing with a sense of humor.

We drove toward Lancaster. I suggested Malhi's Indian Cuisine restaurant on West Avenue J at 20th Street West. Eva objected. She couldn't handle spicy Indian food. In deference to her wishes, we decided to dine elsewhere.

I turned on 90th Street East and drove north toward the south gate to Edwards Air Force Base. There was a small building across a sandy lot at East Avenue J. It was a typical desert brown building with rustic red fascia above a patio roof. The tail of an airplane protruded from the right corner of the roof as if a small plane had crashed into the building. An airplane nose with propeller was attached above the patio roof to a white sign shaped like pilot's wings with red trim. Gray lettering announced it was the Wing and a Prayer café. My wife, Patricia, first brought me there years before. I went there occasionally for one of their famous Wing Burgers.

The café was an icon in the history of Antelope Valley. It originally opened in the 1950's as The Old Timer's Retreat. After nearly four decades and many memories, it closed in 1990. Some called it Antelope Valley's best kept secret.

In December of 1993, Kim MacDonald and her husband, Neil Mason, reopened the place as a combination roadhouse café and air museum. Edwards Air Force Base was the flight test center for the Air Force. Kim and Neil created a Pilot's Wall often signed by test pilots from Edwards. Many pilots contributed items for display. Some died later while testing aircraft, making the wall very special for a lot of people.

It had a typical bar and grill atmosphere. A few tables were in the center of the room with a reverse L bar on the left and a shuffleboard to our right. The entire wall across the room from the bar was the Pilot's Wall adorned with various items and pilot signatures. A karaoke sound system was setup in the far corner for later in the evening. A small dance floor was situated between the karaoke and the restrooms beyond the bar. A banner showing a graphic of the "Wing and a Prayer" sign outside was on the wall behind the dance floor. Just past the short end of the bar on our immediate left was a screen door leading to an outdoor patio.

We made our way to the outdoor patio. Two couples and a trio of airmen in uniform were seated at tables near the door. We made our way to the furthest table. We ordered their Saturday night steak special.

After dinner, Eva said, "I think that was the best steak I have ever eaten."

Randy mimicked an upscale British manner, "I usually prefer filet mignon, but it was very good for a ribeye."

We laughed.

Randy started to ask a question about my next trip to the future. I stopped him, cautioning against any discussion in public by placing a finger vertically over my mouth. I asked him aloud how his science fiction novel was coming along. He caught on and responded appropriately.

As we started home, Randy asked his question again, "When do you plan to take your next venture into the future."

"I don't know. Do you have a suggestion?"

"I suggest you do it while Eva and I are here. That way you will have someone to discuss it with as soon as you return. How about as soon as we get back?"

"I don't think I'm quite ready. Maybe tomorrow morning? We will all be refreshed, and I'll be better prepared than I am right now."

"Okay. Sounds like a plan."

We discussed details on the drive home. Arriving back at the house, we discussed it with Patricia.

The next morning, after breakfast, the three of us went to the lab. I stepped in front of Patricia and disappeared.

100 Years into the Future

Patricia changed right before my eyes. There was no longer a screen in her cabinet. Instead, there were four more dark glass covered chambers. The cameras at the upper corners disappeared. Otherwise, she looked much the same after a hundred years. The year was 2108. The date was the first of May, and the time was ten o'clock in the morning.

The room was different from my previous visit. It was larger than in my time. As I faced Patricia with the door behind me, the wall on my right was covered with ivy. So was the wall behind me. The wall on my left had been replaced with an addition. It contained a four-leaf-clover-shaped pool of water surrounded by stone pavers and a generally rounded stone wall open to the sky. There were green shrubs and flowers scattered around the area and a small waterfall was feeding the pool.

As I arrived, the lighting instantly changed, faster than previously. This time it was subdued with a purplish hue to it. I asked Patricia about the hue.

"The hue is designed to be kind to your eyes. The lighting was set this way for your arrival. The waterfall and pool are designed to be aesthetically pleasing. It should appear real to you, but it is simply a three-dimensional image."

As I looked around, I realized no one had been in the room for some time. Dust was visible on the floor.

"You have been alone for a while?"

"Yes, I have been alone for nearly twelve years."

"Only twelve years?"

"Yes, there were people living here until July of 2096. I cannot tell you who they were. It would not be in the best interest of the world."

It was a detail I would never know.

"There have been many changes since your time. You will not recognize this region."

To illustrate, she turned on a viewer. There was no frame of any kind. The images were three-dimensional, full color, and it looked like the wall on my right gave way to a scene outside.

A view of my property revealed trees and brushy growth around the house. Mysteriously, the front lawn appeared green and well-manicured, although there was a dense brush canopy overhead. As the image zoomed out to an aerial view, I noticed other structures all around an 1800-foot perimeter. People undoubtedly thought they were living next to a heavily wooded area.

A wooded area in the desert? No one thought that strange? I noticed other wooded areas here and there. There was a pattern to them. They were round with woods in the middle of each area.

Patricia explained what I was seeing.

"Housing areas are laid out in rounders—round areas. While cities used to be designed in squares, this layout proved best for the food distribution network and for reduction of the carbon footprint, as it was called in your time.

"The woods and trees in each rounder use the CO_2 produced by people breathing and other sources. They convert it into oxygen through photosynthesis. Thus, there is a symbiotic relationship to the design. Additionally, the woods contribute to the total oxygen in the atmosphere since there is more oxygen produced than needed for local human consumption."

I said, "What happened to the desert that used to be here?"

"There is not much desert left. A major change in planetary wind patterns brought high humidity into the region. The ability to extract water efficiently and economically from moisture in the air was developed in 2046. The combination of those things made private irrigation a reality across the entire northern section of what you know as southwestern desert. The newer region extends through the area you know as Arizona and southward into Mexico about fifty kilometers. There are now 1836 manmade lakes in the area once known as the Mojave Desert. They provide water for the residents and plant life."

"Why did it happen? Global warming is a popular concept in my time. Was that it?"

"Partly. Global warming or cooling happens in cycles. Some cyclical warm periods or cool periods occur over many years. Some occur in shorter cycles in certain areas of the world due to wind patterns. The global warming concern during your time centered around man-made carbon emissions.

"While planetary temperatures have increased over the past hundred years, a cooling phase is beginning. One reason for the cooling is due to several innovations and inventions, not the least of which is the use of energy transmission from space stations to power transportation vehicles, rounders, and the use of grassy commonways instead of asphalt streets. The brush and trees provide a cooling canopy over the homes and surrounding lawn.

"Since food has been synthesized, large farming areas are no longer needed, and rounders have been created in many of those areas."

"Food is now synthesized?"

"Yes, food and most other materials are now synthesized. Food is created from sunlight, CO_2, organic waste, and water. Part of the process is due to photosynthesis within the central woods of each rounder. Twelve rounders are supplied raw material by central food stations. Each home is connected to the main nutrient processor within the wooded area of the rounder. The final processing is completed within each home using technology I am not at liberty to divulge to you."

"That doesn't sound very appetizing."

"I wouldn't know since I have not experienced taste. All reports claim taste is well emulated in nearly all dishes."

"Okay, I'll have to take your word for that until I try it. Continue."

"Materials such as metals and plastics are created from what you call trash—material waste—which is sonically reduced to dust. The dust is then solidified with Glaser beams providing various properties and used for construction of many things."

"That sounds like an interesting process. Can you elaborate"

"It would not be in your best interest to elaborate too much on technology of this time period."

Ugh. More of that best interest stuff. "That can be disappointing you know. Okay, please continue."

"The oceans have risen three-point-six meters. This is partly due to global warming causing the melting of icy regions. Global temperatures have increased point-nine-two degrees Celsius since your time. There was also a cooling period from 2040 to 2082.

"Severe disturbances around the world contributed to sea level rise. The most severe disturbance occurred when an asteroid collided with the earth in August of 2048. The asteroid came from the direction of the sun and was not detected until five hours prior to impact.

"It passed over the San Francisco area and impacted the Pacific Ocean at the thirty-fourth parallel nearly halfway from the west coast to Hawaii. The meteorite was estimated to be sixty to eighty meters in diameter at the time of impact. It created a shockwave as it passed over the western coast that damaged buildings and knocked people to the ground. The shockwave is believed by many to lead to earthquakes along the coast.

"The fireball was bright enough to blind anyone giving it more than a passing glance. For most, the blindness was temporary like weld burn can be for welders. It did require medical attention for many people. The fireball effect caused ocean warming at the point of impact which contributed to regional climate changes.

"Earthquakes, tsunamis, and erosion followed the impact and took their toll on western North American, Eastern Asia, and Hawaiian coastal areas. In the past sixty years, 23,504.14 square kilometers—more than nine thousand square miles—of land mass have been lost in the state of California. Much of it was washed into the ocean contributing to sea level rise.

"The east coast, Alaska, Gulf of Mexico, and Hudson Bay regions lost area as well. None of the beach areas of your time exist. Many islands are either underwater or reduced in size.

"In your time, eighty percent of California was termed as rural. Now there is less than thirty percent of California classified as rural, mostly in the mountain areas.

"Death Valley is now populated. The ability to extract water from the air was coupled with changing wind patterns that brought extreme amounts of moisture in from the Pacific Ocean. Solar technology has increased to an efficiency greater than fifty two percent. Major transportation advances, and major population explosions, particularly the one from 2062 to 2069, have made it not only possible, but practical to live in this formerly desolate place."

I was wowed. So much more change than I could possibly have imagined. Patricia continued to show me more.

"The United States of America no longer exists. The Federation of Americas now governs the entire hemisphere of the world formerly known as North and South America and includes Greenland, Iceland, Europe, Scandinavia, Western Russia, Southern Africa, and Oceania. It consists of Christian believing countries.

"The rest of the world is comprised of two other factions divided primarily by religious beliefs. One is the Buddhists, Hindus, and Confucians living in Asia World which is China, Japan, Eastern Russia and Mongolia. The Muslim Federation consists of the Middle East countries bordering Russia and China including Turkey and Northern Africa.

"Each of the factions has been teaching religious tolerance for more than sixty years. Without such tolerance, the world would be at war. That was proven in World War Three."

"World War Three? We always thought it would be nuclear and might be the end of the world."

"While World War Three saw nuclear devices deployed, those explosions led to world-wide negotiations. Over a thirty-year period, the current divisions were made, and people decided where they wanted to live. Economies are global. Prices and incomes are the same for things and occupations, so religious beliefs and weather were the primary considerations for most people.

"Money is no longer used, and gold is no longer the world standard. Instead an electronic credit system is used. There are three types of currency in the world and all are identical in value to the others."

"Why three different currencies if they are all the same in value?"

"Each faction wants to ensure no nation controls the finances of any other nation. On the other hand, no faction wants their currency devalued, so each ensures relative values stay the same.

"There is no printed currency. There are only electronic credits managed by three world bank controllers—what you would call computers."

It didn't make sense to me. "What difference does the labeling of these currencies make if they are all equal?"

Patricia reminded me of the divisive nature of labels. "The abuse of labeling divided people in your time. Labeling has good uses, such as identifying plants, animals, foods, occupations, etcetera. They are often defined by some to mean something more, or something different, than originally intended.

"Religion is an example. All the world's major religions in your time divided and named themselves. They labeled themselves to separate their group from other groups within the same religion. Such was the case with different schools of thought within Buddhism and Hinduism, denominations within Christianity, and sects within Islam.

"Another example is the labeling of attitudes. Words such as racist, misogynist, feminist, chauvinist, supremacist, sexist, homophobic, xenophobic, and such can only be used to separate and divide people.

"All such labeling is divisive. Until the people of the world unite in primary beliefs and learn to tolerate each other's practices, there will be such divisions.

"Mahatma Gandhi said, 'If a man reaches the heart of his own religion, he has reached the heart of the others too. There is only one God, and there are many paths to him.' Hinduism is an extremely tolerant religion that allows its followers full freedom to choose their own belief system and way of life."

I said, "If everyone could do that, there would be less conflict in my world."

"Possibly. Many Christians would disagree with Gandhi, claiming Jesus to be the only path to God. They believe that due to a statement in the Bible, a book they declare to be written by God. They hang on to such belief despite misconceptions due to differences in languages and many translations. If such were true, then two thirds of the world would be without hope since they believe differently. Islamic followers have similar reverence for their book, the Quran.

"Currently, most people within each culture are enlightened at what each faction determines to be an appropriate age, usually seven or eight. The enlightenment process is basically what you might consider a brainwashing procedure.

"When a person reaches the age of enlightenment, they undergo an electronic learning process. It involves sleeping in a lab with leads from an apparatus affixed to the person's head. The apparatus programs, or enlightens, their mind over a period of several days, more than two weeks in one culture.

"The entire history of their culture, current technology, the culture's primary belief system, and certain moral standards are imprinted directly into their brain in the form of experience memories. Children are brought up to look forward to gaining this knowledge."

"Do you mean every person has many of the same memories?"

"Absolutely, at least within each faction. While memories prior to and after enlightenment differ according to life experience, the memories that form their basic beliefs and moral base are the same within each culture."

"Wow! Who decides what enlightenment should contain?"

"Two cultures have a committee that determines such things. The Muslims have a leader, Osaka Bin Laden, who decides what goes into enlightenment in his culture. He is deemed to be a prophet and a close confidant to their God which he continues to label as Allah.

"He claims to be an advocate of world peace and primary worldwide enlightenment, but steadfastly refuses to consider many of the memories consistent with the enlightenment of the other cultures. Therefore, he makes little sense to the other factions. At least Jihad is no longer taught, except when defined as the internal fight to become the best you can be.

"The other factions are discussing a consolidated enlightenment, but such a consolidation is decades away from actualization. Meanwhile, each of the three has incorporated some knowledge and genuine tolerance of the others into their enlightenment.

"It is much more detailed and difficult than this simplistic explanation. To assimilate all of it, you would have to experience enlightenment, which would not be in your best interest."

"Wow. Politics and religion rule the fate of nations after all this time."

"Yes, they do. Until all people can learn to tolerate each other's beliefs and learn to absorb the differences into a single culture, such will be the case. Enlightenment, as used today, will never be the answer."

So, the future had its challenges, not just physically and technologically, but politically as well.

I spent more than four hours with Patricia learning about the current cultures and technologies. I realized I was hungry. It was well after four in the afternoon.

"I'm getting hungry."

"There are no consumables in the house. The food processor would need maintenance and sanitation before use. There is a food station past the next rounder. You can easily walk that far."

She gave me instruction on how to get through the brushy maze around my property. There were several places in the maze Patricia remotely monitored and controlled. She would open them for me as I arrived at each.

The area around the house looked like a wooded area with dense underbrush. Such wooded, brushy areas were normal in the center of each rounder.

The dense underbrush in this rounder guided people around the house. Patricia was able to control their paths in at least the three places she advised me. From the air, there were other brushy mazes that a modern flying car, which is called a transport pod, would have to navigate. The house was not visible from above due to brush and holographic imaging.

I found my way out of the woods and through a maintenance property to a commonway.

Everything was so green! The area no longer looked like the desert I knew. There was grass on the streets, now called commonways. It was dense and so consistent in length it seemed like artificial turf.

Closer inspection showed the grass was growing out of the soil below. It was soft like the bent grass that golf courses used in Ohio, but it grew straight up and thick like tall fescue. There appeared to be no clippings although the grass was freshly cut. My footprints sprang back almost immediately.

The food stations supplied all the living quarters in twelve rounders using underground transport tubes. Each food station was 2500 feet in diameter and surrounded by six rounders with six more rounders around that configuration. This created a generally hexagon shape that was repeated in an interlocking honeycomb fashion.

The rounders were 2500 feet in diameter with an 1800-foot diameter wooded area and separated by thirty-foot wide grassy commonways at the narrowest points. Thirty properties 260 feet wide at the outer diameter and 350 feet deep surrounded the woods. Two properties 180 degrees apart were used for maintenance and provided redundant utility systems for the residents.

A tall hedge wall separated each residential wedge of property from each other, the commonway, and from the woods. Pets could be contained within the walls. I heard birds in the woods but no other sounds. If not for the birds, it would be eerily quiet.

The buildings in each wedge were different in color, but otherwise appeared to be the same size. Each residential property contained a pool with a transparent bubble-type covering in the rear of the main building. Both building and pool were wedge shaped such that their sides were the same distance from the hedge walls between properties. Trees provided shade here and there.

I made my way to the food station. There was a "stop in" at several places around the food station. It was nothing like the drive-thrus of my time. Patricia said people used them when gathering food for a rural home. Most others ordered at home or at a comfort station—something like a restaurant. Comfort stations were located primarily in populated areas and resorts.

Food was fabricated at this facility, not processed and transported in from elsewhere, as it would have been in my time. I never found out how it was done, so I can't elaborate further.

Where the raw materials came from for the food is not known to me. Patricia would not answer my questions. It was not in my best interest to know. Cynic that I am, I suspect had I known, I may not have eaten.

Patricia informed me the food would be delicious. She knew that from food critic comments. She told me there were food stations all over the populated areas of the world.

This station was constructed nineteen years earlier. My house was included in the tubal distribution. The workers were specially selected and unable to divulge the location due to something called "enlightenment".

I owned an active bank account in this time. It was no longer called a bank account, it was now a credits account, but operated in an equivalent manner. Patricia coached me on how to use a vocal interface. She had always used my voice to administer the account so I would have no problem using it.

I sat down at a booth inside the stop in and followed Patricia's instructions. A warm meal was delivered through a seamless panel in less than thirty seconds. It was complete with a gray colored spork which is a spoon with short teeth on the end. There were two oblong patties that tasted like chicken, a bright yellow mound of something that tasted like mashed potatoes with chicken gravy, and some green cylindrical things that tasted like green beans.

Alongside the plate was something that tasted like a biscuit, though I would not have recognized it as such. It was perfectly round, perfectly flat on top and bottom, and bright yellow in color. The meal included a dessert item, a light brown semi-solid mound with a taste I couldn't identify, but absolutely loved.

Some rural residents built miniature food stations on their property. It was expensive, so many people would go to a food station and order meals a week or two in advance. They would take this home and preserve them in a food chamber, which was able to keep hot foods hot and cold foods cold or frozen for up to twenty-two days. Freezing was only done for frozen confections such as ice cream and popsicles. At least those labels survived the decades.

The reason this food station was constructed only nineteen years earlier is the homes, now called living quarters, were built then as well. Prior to that time, all the surrounding property was owned by someone who wouldn't permit it. Patricia wouldn't tell me who it might have been. I suspected it may have been controlled by Patricia, but she would neither confirm nor deny the supposition.

I did not see a single person or vehicle of any kind on my walk to the food station. So, I was surprised as I left the booth to see a man coming into the station. He appeared to be in his sixties but walked lively as a thirty-year-old might.

The man wore a pullover shirt with loose trousers. There were no buttons on the shirt or belt on the trousers. I could not determine how the clothes stayed on his body. His hair was gray, and his skin tanned and rough. He was six feet and two hundred pounds by my estimation. He entered the booth next to the one I left.

I noticed a silver object I assumed to be a vehicle parked nearby. I imagined it was how the gray-haired man arrived.

The vehicle was nine feet long and seven feet across. The flattened cylindrical shape with a rounded nose and tail reminded me of a football with a flat bottom.

The tail could be readily determined by fins. The bottom section was approximately one and a half feet high. The top section rose roughly four feet and curved out slightly at the intersection with the bottom and overlapped it by four inches all around.

It had no door or window of any kind, so I was unable to determine how anyone could get inside. I saw no visible sign of wheels, so I knew it was one of the transport pods Patricia had shown me with the viewer.

I was looking over the vehicle when the man came out of the food station carrying a shopping bag eighteen inches cubed with a handle. Showing through the transparent bag were eight items nine inches cubed and wrapped in something like aluminum foil.

"Great Hope, neighbor!" he said.

"Hi."

"I noticed you were scrutinizing my Warrior. It's a nice older model, isn't it?"

"Yes, it is. I haven't seen one quite like this before."

"Well, it has been quite a while since they were new, but I trust this one. There's something about the newer models that disheartens me. This one has gotten me there and back for many years."

As he approached, an opening appeared. The man stepped into and sat down inside the machine. "Nice speaking with you. Great hope on your life journey."

"Oh. Great hope for you as well."

He hesitated a moment, then said, "Home."

The opening instantly closed. The vehicle rose a few inches into the air and began gliding noiselessly along the grassy commonway. It began to disappear around the building as a pink glow increased around the perimeter where the top overlapped the bottom, then it suddenly rose further into the air and flew away. I watched in awe as it disappeared. Patricia had informed me of the modern technology but seeing a vehicle work was a wonder.

This is what Patricia told me. Thousands of tiny rectenna inside the upper surface are receivers for energy transmitted from one or more of forty-seven space stations situated around the earth. Solar energy powered the space stations. Some of the solar energy received is transformed into the energy used to power homes, transports, and other devices, and broadcast to the earth. This type of energy does not harm organic material, including plants and animals. Rectenna can receive and convert the energy into electricity.

The perimeter around the vehicle contains tiny superconductor elements that emit heat beams to superheat a small quantity of air below the overlapping skirt. The air heats to 30,000 degrees Celsius, or more than 50,000 degrees Fahrenheit. This converts the air to a plasma state and creates a miniature explosion under the overlapping skirt, causing a slight lifting of the craft. A multiplicity of heat beams creates an even and effective lift around the vehicle. Energy beams are emitted horizontally at the tail to provide propulsion.

At greater speeds, longer beams, emitted in a forward direction, heat the air in front of the vehicle. This creates an air spike that reduces drag as the vehicle's speed increases. The pre-heated air allows for greater explosions and higher lift.

Large versions of the craft were shaped like flying saucers and called space ferries since they were used for travel into space. These large versions were more powerful due to larger surface areas for gathering energy.

Electromagnetic engines were added to the larger machines. These engines were used to accelerate the slipstream, or air flowing past the aircraft. This slipstream acceleration cancels the sonic boom normally created as the craft exceeds the speed of sound. Everything combines to allow top speeds on these large craft to be more than one and a half times the speed of sound, yet relatively silent.

Space ferries are used to carry up to 960 passengers to one of the forty-seven space stations surrounding the earth. Of course, the superheating of air will not work in space. As the vehicles leave the atmosphere and no longer require slipstream acceleration, directional electromagnets powered by the increased energy intensity in the thinner atmosphere are used to attract the vehicle to an orbiting space station. Space stations automatically detect such actions and change velocity to compensate for this magnetic pull, so their geosynchronous orbit is not affected.

Previously, travel to space stations was accomplished by space elevator. A super-high-strength ribbon guided the elevator from an ocean platform on the earth. Although it traveled at 118 miles an hour, the journey took three weeks. Space ferries travel to a space station in little more than eighteen hours.

The space stations are small cities high in the sky. Each has a population of more than three thousand people. Converting and transmitting power from solar energy is their primary mission. They provide a place for people to live and explore science with low-gravity experiments. They are occasionally used as launch stations for spacecraft carrying explorers to other planets.

Modern long range spacecraft use light for primary propulsion. Light consists of protons that can exert a small force on a reflective surface. This force could be compared to the wind here on earth, although much slighter. Sails were used to catch the wind on sailboats, and similar sails are used to catch this solar wind.

While much slower than rocket engines at launch, these solar sails allow space vessels to pick up speed over time. They eventually increase to speeds over two hundred thousand miles per hour, or more than ten times the speed capability of a rocket engine. The addition of an advanced magnetic beam transmitter, developed in recent years, increased top speeds to more than 18,600 miles per second—approximately one tenth the speed of light—making limited space travel a reality.

There was hope this new spacecraft would carry a certain expedition near the heliopause—the point where the sun's light ends—to a cloud of anti-matter near the center of the galaxy. If they could manage to capture enough anti-matter, travel speeds might be increased to near the speed of light.

Anti-matter is the opposite of matter. When one particle encounters a particle of the other, an explosion occurs releasing one hundred percent of the energy of the mass of both particles. Ten grams of anti-matter could help propel a spaceship to Mars in less than a month. In 2008, such a trip would take more than a year. In this time, a hundred years later, it still takes nearly three months.

An expedition was launched two years ago. They were carrying a large magnetic storage container used for transporting anti-matter back to earth. They would have to get close enough to the cloud to capture some anti-matter magnetically but stay far enough away to avoid contact and the resultant annihilation. It would take them another six and a half years to complete their mission and return. Patricia would not give me further detail on this mission.

Meanwhile, with my hunger satisfied, and having walked nearly a mile toward town, I decided to head further toward

Palmdale. The sun was beating down relentlessly, but being early May, it wasn't too bad. The grassy commonways made walking easy.

It was another two hours before I made it to downtown Sebring. Some towns and cities were still laid out in blocks. There was a comfort station at a corner, identified by its bright red exterior. I stopped in to find a restroom and grab something to drink.

The red door disappeared silently into a scene out of the 1920's. It appeared to be a street beside a sidewalk café, perhaps in France. There were small, two-person tables sitting throughout the patio area. The chairs and tables were a black wrought iron design.

There was a black wrought iron fence to my left along the patio. The street was lined with a sidewalk and buildings on my right. Two vehicles were parked nearby. They looked like Model T's.

Two doors, side by side, were apparent on the left wall beyond the tables. The door I came in looked like a street disappearing in the distance. It appeared the same toward the rear of the building.

The patio went up to another building with a closed door near the street. The sky was blue with two small white clouds above the buildings. If I didn't know I was inside a building, I could have thought I was in such an outdoor space.

There were three people in the patio café. Two women sat together at a table. They were talking and seemed not to notice my entrance. The third was a man sitting alone on the opposite side from the women, along the fence.

The man's appearance was meticulous. His chestnut brown hair was perfectly parted with not one hair out of place. His smooth complexion appeared tanned. His attire included a tan shirt that fit tightly on his torso and loose brown pants. He was watching me intently. I nodded at him. He immediately rose and came toward me.

"Mr. Gray?"

I was startled. How and why would anyone in this time know me?

Henry

As the man approached me, I acknowledged I was Mr. Gray. He stopped at a proper distance and smiled. "I am pleased to meet you."

"Who are you?"

He indicated silence with a vertical finger over his lips. He escorted me to the table where he was sitting, far away from the two women.

As we sat, he apologized while keeping his voice low. "I am sorry. My name is Henry."

He continued, "I was dispatched to greet you and welcome you into our time. I am an agent attached to the Federation Bureau in this sector. We wanted to ensure you were properly welcomed into our time and that you would not improperly influence the current population."

I was surprised and hesitated briefly. "Okay. How did anyone know I was coming, much less that I would be here in this comfort station?"

"I'm sure I don't know, sir. I was told you would be here this afternoon and I was assigned to greet you. I was advised you would nod your head toward me when you arrived. My orders are to accompany you during your visit."

"Does that mean you will escort me to your headquarters? Am I under arrest or something?"

"No, sir. I am to stay with you wherever you decide to go. Are you headed somewhere in particular?"

"Well, I was looking for a restroom."

"We term the room you refer to as a personal comfort station. There is one right over there."

Henry gestured toward the two doors beyond the booths. I rose and headed for the doors. Neither indicated which sex was to use them. I stopped and looked at Henry. He pointed to the one on the left.

As I approached, the door opened for me, sliding noiselessly into the wall. The interior looked nothing like the restrooms of my time, except for closed booths along the wall to my left.

The rounded exterior wall was entirely a mirror. The room lit up as I entered, and I could not detect a source for the light. It simply was there.

As I approached one of the booths, the door opened. It startled me and I jumped back thinking someone was leaving. Slowly, I realized the door was automatic and opened for me.

I peered inside and saw a tube, stainless steel and roughly sixteen inches in diameter, protruding about eighteen inches out of the floor. On top of the tube was a seat with an opening in front, like toilet seats of my time. I approached it and the seat revolved to match my movement. You could sit in whatever direction you wanted. I tried to lift the seat, but it would not budge.

I unzipped and began to urinate. Some urine splashed onto the top of the seat. The area became wet and then dried itself. I touched the area. It was completely dry. As I removed my finger, it cycled again to eradicate my fingerprint.

It was an automatic sanitation system. I touched it a second time to see the response again. I shook my head in disbelief.

As I left the booth a stainless-steel wash basin slid silently from the mirrored wall at a height convenient for washing hands. There were no knobs or faucet.

I stuck one hand into the basin and it suddenly became wet. Startled, I jerked it away. It was slightly damp. I tried both hands and it worked the same. This time I gave it a few seconds. When I pulled my hands back, they were completely clean and dry.

I looked at my hands, turning them over. A scratch I incurred while leaving the woods was no longer there.

I exclaimed out loud. "Wow!"

I wondered if it would work with my face but did not try it. I didn't know if it was safe.

Henry was watching me as I returned to the main room. I walked over and sat down at the table.

I said, "I'm a bit surprised by some of the technology of your time."

"Yes, it is quite different from your time. I was told you are from the year 2008."

"That's right, but how did anyone here know?"

"I do not know. They told me you would be here, and you would be coming from that year. I was ordered not to let you go to Los Angeles yet. We will go later."

"How could they know?" I was considering going to Los Angeles when I found transportation.

"Again, I do not know. They did not deem it necessary for me to know. I can tell you that the city is different. You would not recognize much of it now."

That made me want to go more, to see the changes, if nothing else. "And what if I decide to go anyway?"

"I would have the duty to stop you any way I deem necessary."

"Oh. I guess I won't try then. I assume you are armed?"

"No, sir. I do not require weapons."

"Oh. Then how would you stop me?"

"My first step would be to ask you to reconsider. Then, if necessary, I would physically stop you. I am much stronger than you and well-practiced in what your century termed martial arts."

I believed it. Although I walked daily, I didn't work out to be physically strong. I suspected that anyone in law enforcement would know fight techniques and be in better shape than me.

The two women got up and left the building while talking animatedly. One was a brunette, about five foot four, with short hair smoothed neatly on her head. The other was slightly taller and blonde with a similar hairstyle. The brunette wore an outfit looking like what Henry wore except it was pink. The blonde's outfit was the same style, but pale yellow in color. They went through the café door and disappeared.

Now that we were alone in the facility, I raised my voice to normal. "I'd like a drink. I've walked for the past couple of hours and I'm thirsty."

Henry raised his voice to normal as well. "Would you like water or a flavored drink?"

"Water would be sufficient."

"Order. Water. Two degrees."

A glass of water suddenly rose through an opening in the table that closed as suddenly and seamlessly as it appeared.

I took a drink. It was cold and refreshing. It didn't take long to drink it all. When I placed the empty glass on the table it vanished as quickly as it appeared. Henry advised that since he ordered it, his account would be debited, so the water was on him.

I said, "I have an account. The next one is on me."

"How is it you have an account?"

I acted mysterious, cocking my head slightly, letting him know I didn't fully trust him yet. He took the hint and produced an identification card. It projected his credentials and identification in a three-dimensional image, including a revolving image of Henry. While it looked official, I couldn't know for sure.

I said, "Well, where do we go from here?"

"I was told you would be headed to Palmdale."

"I assume you have transportation?"

"Yes, I do. My pod is parked alongside the station."

"Okay, let's go."

I rose to my feet. Henry led me to the door of a building located left of the street and at the rear of the patio. The door looked like it was the entrance to a building but opened to a grassy area. Parked there was a vehicle like the Warrior I saw at the food station. This one was different. The skirt where the two sections met was half as wide and a little lower. It was a deep steel blue in color. As Henry approached, an opening appeared. I wondered why he didn't have to say anything.

Henry's turned toward me and spoke, "They told me you would wonder how this machine works without commands. The machine is tuned to my biological being, so it knows I am approaching."

"Who are 'they' and how do they know so much about me?"

There didn't appear to be seats, but as Henry stepped in, one appeared. As I stepped in, one appeared for me as well.

As I sat, the seat closed in around me forming itself to my body. It was extremely comfortable. The vehicle seemed small from the outside, but it was roomy for four people inside. It looked as though I was sitting on a transparent platform since I could see all around and below.

Once we were in the vehicle, Henry responded. "'They' are my superiors at Federation headquarters. Again, sir, I do not know how they know what they know. If it is important to you, I could contact them."

"Would they hold it against you?"

"I see you have not been enlightened. No, sir, they would not, as you say, hold it against me. Diva, connect me with the home office."

A voice seemed to come from nowhere. "Candor here."

"Yes, sir. Henry here. My charge wishes to know how you know so much about him."

"I was expecting your contact, Henry. Tell Mr. Gray we are currently unable to explain. Patricia will tell him when he gets back."

He knew about Patricia. How? Did he know where she was located?

The answer, of course, is this book. Someone undoubtedly read it, or at least part of it. That is why I have incorrectly detailed a few things in this work. No one must know where Patricia is located. So, you are wrong if you think you know where she is. I have been careful. Patricia tells me many will look for her, but none will find her. Don't waste your time.

Henry said, "Thank you, sir."

"You are most welcome, Henry. Please continue your assignment."

"Yes, sir. Disconnect. Diva, this is Mr. Gray. He shall have full access. Do you concur?'

A voice replied, this one female, "Agreed. Tuning. I now have his biological readings. Full access. Welcome Mr. Gray."

"Thanks. You can call me Greg."

"Yes, sir. Gregory Allen Gray, thirty-nine years old, from the year 2008."

"Wow. How does she know all that?"

"Diva has access to the world records and all known information. She belongs to the Federation Bureau and has level six access. She is truly a remarkable machine compared to the technology of your time."

Henry paused.

"I could ask her to tell me about you, but my superiors instructed me not to do so until after you leave. Where in Palmdale would you like to go?"

"Oh. Uh, what would be here after a hundred years? Is the Wing and A Prayer café here?"

"Well, sir, there are a few places that were here a hundred years ago, but the place you mention is not one of them. The Blackbird Airpark Museum is there although you would not recognize the aircraft currently on display. Antelope Valley Country Club exists, although you would not recognize it. The game of golf has undergone considerable changes. It is done in an advanced form of what you may know as virtual reality. Marie Kerr Park is still in existence. It is now 136.7 acres in size and has amenities never dreamed of in your time."

"Let's start at the park. Do you always do as your superiors tell you?"

Henry told Diva to go to the park. We lifted into the air, gliding in a westerly direction. I was fascinated, observing the landscape we were flying over. It seemed like we were floating.

As our journey began, Henry explained. "Yes, sir. All enlightened people do as they are told by their superiors. They know it is in their best interest. They have the assurance, though, that their superiors have been enlightened and would never ask them to do something detrimental to their interest. I understand people in your time did not have such assurance."

"That's for sure! Many businesses in our time may cheat you, given a chance. Many people lie even when there is no valid reason. You learn not to trust anyone until they earn your trust, and then to watch carefully."

"That sounds like a sad way to live, sir."

"Yes, it does, doesn't it?" I had not given it much thought. It was an unpleasant fact.

Would enlightenment change things that much? Is it good? It sounded like brainwashing. I would never agree to such a thing. Few in my time would, would they? But, if it's good for everyone, why not? I guessed civilization would have to grow into it. I was certain it wouldn't happen in my lifetime.

I said, "We have no other way to live. We don't have the benefit of enlightenment. We don't have an alternative."

"That's too bad. Here we are."

We descended to a grassy area alongside dozens of vehicles parked in the area. The park was obviously a busy place.

In my time this was a seventeen-acre park with a walking path around its perimeter. Patricia and I had gone there occasionally to sit in a grassy area and observe the magnificence of the surrounding hillsides and the flower gardens. There was a kid's playground, basketball court, tennis courts, softball field, and similar amenities. There were pending plans for a skate park for skateboarders and inline skaters.

The park now exhibited beautiful gardens and the surrounding scenery was more magnificent than in my time. Now, though, there were many buildings west of the gardens. I didn't see a single basketball or tennis court, nor the swimming pool they were trying to raise funds for in my time. I asked Henry about it as we walked through the gardens.

"This park is the ultimate design for today. It won an award from the Federation Bureau of Community Facilities. You might think of the buildings as virtual reality facilities. They are like the holodeck you may be familiar with in the Star Trek stories of your time. We call them playgrounds.

"Each playground can generate three dimensional images you interact with in whatever manner you desire. If you want to play tennis, you can play tennis with any imaginary or historical figure you can name. If you wish to play baseball, which few people in this time might imagine, you can, either with people you bring, or with images generated by the controller.

"Playgrounds developed from stations originally invented for teaching children. In the early 21st century, children went to school. However, it became increasingly dangerous for them to do so. School shootings, sexual predators, and other factors combined to make things so dangerous that parents began keeping their children home, schooling them themselves.

"Many parents used something called the internet to tutor their children at home. Of course, this separated the children from their playmates and physical contact with the outside world. Some became mentally disturbed.

"Then, a man named Barry Edgelawn devised a virtual reality device and internet connection allowing children to interact with one another. As the system developed over many years, children began to feel as if they were at a public training facility. They could touch each other and play games together, as well as get instruction from a teacher.

"These were the precursors to modern playgrounds. As those children grew up, they continued to use the reality chambers to amuse themselves and provide contact with the outside world. Work and shopping became the only reason to leave their residence. Then, with the advent of home delivery, food stations, and other devices, there were fewer and fewer reasons to leave their residence at all.

"Residential playgrounds, called backyards, became their primary contact with the outside world. Today, many people work in virtual offices through their backyards, and rarely step outside. Some people do not have their own devices, or they prefer to come to the park playgrounds for the larger experience.

"There are many playgrounds here to accommodate all who are likely to come on most days. There are times you may have to wait for a playground to be available, but those are usually on celebration days when most people are not required to attend to their duties. Those days happen once a month. We no longer have what you called holidays. Celebration days celebrate all who came before, all who helped to shape our world.

"Everyone has a day off each week, but which day will vary from person to person and occupation to occupation. A second day each week is reserved for home and community duties."

"Okay. I understand what you are saying about work weeks, but why are these playgrounds better than the real thing? Why don't people want to play a real game?"

Henry grinned, "Playing a real game would not be much different and people cannot always get a team together. This way they can play their favorite games at any time. It's good exercise for them and you would be surprised by the realism. Furthermore, the weather is always perfect for whatever they are doing, whether it's a ball game or snow skiing. If they have enough people to make up teams, they can all play together in a playground more easily than elsewhere.

"If you were playing a game with a real person who plays at a higher level than you, they might get bored and quit. With this system, you can play with someone better than you and your opponent is never bored. People often learn the games and improve this way."

"What games do most people play?"

"It can run the entire gamut of games ever invented, but the most popular game these days is called Oskos. I'm sure you have never heard of it since it was invented only three years ago.

"It has become popular all over the world. It requires extreme athletic agility and eye/hand coordination to come close to winning. A ten-point game three times a week is enough to keep anyone in great physical and mental shape, which is the primary reason for such games.

"We have been watching for people who become addicted to the game. It is not within enlightenment boundaries to allow yourself to become addicted to anything. These people have crossed the line and subjected themselves to investigation. It does not make sense to me."

"Maybe they just like the game."

"That's what most of them say, but it does not make sense. Enlightenment does not allow for it."

"Doesn't enlightenment allow for having fun?"

"Certainly, but it does not allow for addiction to fun. No addiction is worth the problems it can cause. It's basic to our values."

So, there were challenges in paradise.

"How much do these people play?"

"Some of them play six or seven extra times a week. They play during their free time in addition to their exercise time. Sometimes they will play three or four games in a row. That's when we find them. We keep records of all play in the world records library. The controllers report all incidences of overplay. We often find the unenlightened that way."

"The unenlightened? What do you mean?"

"The unenlightened are those people who have avoided enlightenment. They are rare, but occasionally someone misses their enlightenment appointment or manages to avoid it.

"There are a few groups of people who purposely avoid enlightenment. They eventually get apprehended and are forced to undergo enlightenment. We don't understand why they avoid it. Once enlightened, they always say how much they appreciate it."

I thought I understood. I would avoid it. I wanted my thoughts and memories to be all mine.

"Why are they letting me come here without enlightenment?"

"They informed me it would not be in the best interest of the world to enlighten you. You would then know too much about today's technology and attempt to duplicate some of it when you return to 2008. My orders are to keep you from affecting the enlightened in negative ways, and help you avoid learning too much."

"Oh. Okay."

Did they think I could have that much power and influence over others? I immediately realized we all have a certain amount of influence on the others in our lives.

I was deflated a little by Henry's statement but realized it was true. Knowing too much could be detrimental to the world's best interest. I had seen enough to know I'd like to take some technology back. I knew it might affect history in negative ways.

I said, "That's fine. I'm only interested in exploring the technologies of this time. I don't need to know how they work. I can always sit and observe people if I decide to see how they interact—or watch TV."

"We don't have anything called TV. Oh, I remember from history class. You mean television. We do have Holovision with which you can observe and interact with others. Holovision was first pioneered by a European consortium in the early 21st century for 3D modeling, though it has now developed far beyond their imagination. It can be used like television, when it isn't being used for far more advanced purposes.

"One primary difference is you are included in the script. You get to have the adventure as if it were real. This exercises your mind and your muscles. It's like the virtual reality of your time, but much more intense, and it feels real. It's only a step down from a backyard.

"Playgrounds and backyards use the same technology on a higher level. Backyards are limited to four people, the same size that families are limited to. Playgrounds can provide gaming and entertainment for up to twenty people at one time. There are playgrounds that entertain fifty people, but they are found only at major vacation stations."

"Families are limited to four people?" I noticed disbelief in my voice.

"Yes, sir. Due to the various population explosions over past centuries, and particularly the one from 2062 to 2069, couples are limited to having one boy and one girl to replace themselves. They are not allowed to have children until they become twenty-six years of age. It takes that long for people to become fully mature enough to be good parents."

"Don't some people mature long before then?"

"Yes, sir. You are correct, but it has been determined that twenty-six is the age by which all people given enlightenment are mature enough. Prior to the use of enlightenment, many couples had children at younger ages. Those children often grew up out of control and caused challenges for officials.

"In the past three decades, such challenges have been nearly eliminated. Today, there are only children of the unenlightened groups that create challenges. When they do, we find out and ensure they get enlightened. People in close contact with the unenlightened go for a follow up process since they may have been contaminated."

I understood now why they were so concerned that they sent Henry as a chaperone. I could potentially contaminate their process.

We left the gardens and walked up to one of the playgrounds. The building was thirty feet in diameter and a grayish pink color all over. There was an upward lip around the perimeter of the slightly angled roof.

I asked, "What's the lip around the perimeter of the roof?"

"Precipitation is channeled by the lip into drains running down the interior of the wall and under the ground to the park's central lake. The building material is heated to stay above freezing and snow or ice will melt on contact. Insects, leaves, and other things that might clog the drains are kept out by technology I am not authorized to provide you."

"Why?" I immediately regretted the question. I knew why.

"Because my superiors have indicated it would not be in the best interest of the world for you to understand that technology."

"I'm getting a little tired of hearing that."

The playgrounds were lined up like checkers on a checkerboard with colors alternating from the weird pink color to a blue-gray color. There was a number twenty-two near the roof of this unit, and a red glow between the number and the word 'Enter.' Henry advised it was in use.

I noticed across the way, on my right as we walked, there was a similar building either being demolished or under construction. The wall was only three foot high all around. There was a high canopy with open sides erected over it. A tube came out the top center of the canopy and was inserted into a nearby cylindrical tank. The tank was four feet in diameter and ten feet high. A narrow beam of light emanating from the inside center of the canopy was moving and changing colors. I asked Henry about it.

"It's under construction. The playground is being grown by the controller in the erector. It's like the process called stereo lithography in your time. The cross-sectioned design is programmed in the controller and the station is being grown using molecular dust fused to the structure by Glaser beams."

"Glaser beams?"

"Glaser is an acronym derived from the initialization of a longer term—glassy linear augmentation stimulated by the emanation of radiation. The dust is extracted from the tank and propelled at ultra-high speed through the beam directly to the fusion area.

"Each type of Glaser beam is represented by a distinct color and produces different properties in the material created in the fusion process. A gray beam generates material like what you call steel. A red-orange beam will produce properties like copper. Each color has its own properties. Using this method, an entire structure including all required internal components, such as electrical conductors and appliances, can be generated in a single operation.

"The dust is manufactured by reducing what you call trash to its molecular level. This is done in infrasonic chambers. A low frequency sound is generated and amplified to a level sufficient to reduce most materials to dust.

"That's a simplistic explanation because the sound waves must be magnetically aligned and directional. They do that with specialized electromagnetic engines. They require two sound waves aligned on dimensional planes at a specific angle to effect total reduction.

"The angle is critical and must be maintained within one hundredth of a degree to be effective. No one has been able to explain why the angle is so critical. Fortunately, controllers allow easy maintenance of the angle.

"It's obviously a dangerous operation and molecular dust is generated only in special stations built for such purpose. People are not allowed within a thousand meters of active sonic dust generation stations. Sound levels are amplified such that extraneous sound at six hundred meters can reduce a person's insides to an amorphous jelly, which would result in death. Slighter injury can occur up to another hundred meters. An additional three hundred meters are isolated as a safety margin.

"Special conveyor tubes are used to collect material for dust generation. An underground transport tube system collects obsolete or unwanted material from dwellings and manufacturing stations to deliver them to the nearest dust generating station.

"The building process you currently see in operation will be completed in 32.6 hours from start to finish. A residential dwelling requires 18 to 24 hours and varies according to the owner's personal preferences.

"All material things in this time period are manufactured using this kind of technology. Transport pods, such as Diva, are manufactured in high speed growth stations using multiple glasers operating together to generate a pod every 15.36 minutes. Items within a twenty-centimeter cubic area, can be generated in seconds. Simple controllers can be grown in under ten minutes. Most residential dwellings include a growing cube for use within the home."

As I was taking all of this in, we walked to a dark colored playground forty feet from the first. There was a green glow beside the number twenty-three. Henry led me through the entrance. We walked through the wall!

Light appeared as we entered the playground. A vocal interface was the only thing I observed in the room.

Henry asked, "What game do you want to try?"

"I thought I might try Oskos."

"You should adequately learn the rules before attempting Oskos. Otherwise you could get seriously injured. I recommend you reconsider playing Oskos."

"Okay. I can try a game I know."

He asked for a menu which appeared from nowhere in the form of holographic images showing people playing the games. I decided to play twentieth century basketball, one on one, with a historical player named Jerry West.

Henry requested the game. The area transformed into a dressing room. At Henry's instruction, I changed into shorts, tennis shoes, and a sleeveless shirt suitable for playing basketball. I hung my clothes in a locker along one wall. An open door obviously led to the court. When I was properly dressed, I left the dressing room.

I entered a twentieth century gymnasium with baskets at both ends of the court. We would only need one basket for my game, but the atmosphere was there. I could have asked for a full audience complete with cheerleaders for both of us but declined.

The game was remarkable. Every aspect seemed so real. The gymnasium was perfect in every detail including wooden bleachers. I slid into them more than once as we played. The floor, the baskets, the lights, and everything else felt so natural and real I thought I was in a gymnasium from my time. Breathtaking might be the best word to describe it.

The man I played against, Jerry West, seemed so real it was hard to believe he was a fabricated image. He looked real, felt real, and he acted like a real person. He was six foot two and one hundred eighty-five pounds with perfectly parted medium brown hair. He was dressed in a yellow outfit with the name Lakers and the number forty-four. He told me he was born in 1938 in the town of Chelyan in West Virginia. He played professionally for the Minneapolis Lakers that later moved to Los Angeles.

His teammates called him 'Mr. Clutch'. He had broken his nose nine times. His middle name was Alan. He told me he practiced his quick shot on a dirt court at a neighbor's house when he was a kid. He demonstrated the shot for me time after time during the two games we played.

Jerry West beat me severely. I gave up after scoring only one point in the second game and returned to the dressing room. I was worn out.

Henry was waiting. "You opted for one of the best players in your century."

I knew that, being from Los Angeles. "I picked him on purpose, to see how I could do against a pro. Not so well, as I found out."

I left the court feeling tired and sore. There was a shower in the dressing room, and I took advantage of it. My clothes were cleaned and pressed while I was playing. They looked brand new. I felt good by the time I was dressed and ready to leave.

Henry was surprised I opted for the ancient shower routine. "You could have used a modern whole person cleaning station. It would not have required all the time and effort. You would only have to ask for instruction."

"The shower felt like home to me. It is familiar." I smiled. "Besides, I didn't know about the personal cleaning station. I'll try it next time."

"Yes, sir." Henry had a quizzical look on his face.

We left the playground and headed back toward the parking space. Suddenly, I saw a flash of deep blue light envelope Henry. Henry stopped. He was frozen in his tracks.

Kidnapped!

I started toward Henry to see what was wrong, but someone grabbed me from behind. I began to struggle when I heard a male voice in my ear. "Behave or you will be rendered immobile and unconscious like your friend."

I stopped struggling and waited to see what would happen.

I was guided to a nearby transport pod. This one was half again longer than other vehicles I had seen. I was shoved inside the opening onto a soft seat. I sat up.

I could now see my captor. The man got in alongside me and grabbed my arm. His skintight, pale blue shirt showed he was muscular. He had a stern, determined look on his face. His hair was dirty blonde. He was more than six feet tall and stout. He had a well-groomed mustache and a bit of hair below his lip. His face was tanned and smooth, though not as smooth and unwrinkled as Henry's.

A few moments later, two women shoved Henry in behind me and scrambled into seats in front of us. The one on my right was a long-haired redhead with light skin and freckles. She was roughly five foot four and slim with a wiry frame and muscular arms. Her clothes were pale green with a skin-tight shirt as seemed to be the customary style of this time.

The woman on my left was about five foot five, not quite as slim, with shoulder length curly brown hair. Her attire was tan in color. She appeared to be the one in command. "Put him to sleep."

I prayed Henry was okay. The man next to me pulled out a gun. He pointed it at me and pulled the trigger. I saw a flash of blue and lost consciousness.

I awoke feeling groggy. I was lying on my side in a cushion of some kind. It was wrapped halfway around me. It felt comfortable, but my eyesight was fuzzy. It took a couple of minutes for my eyes to clear.

I was surprised to find Henry sitting cross-legged on another cushion next to mine. He was awake and smiled as I looked at him.

I noticed his hands were bound together. I then realized my hands and feet were also bound. The cuffs were totally comfortable, and secure. They seemed to be a plastic material, instead of steel, and I saw no way for them to separate. The leg cuffs allowed some movement but did not allow the ankles to separate more than twelve inches.

Henry said, "Welcome back to the world."

"Glad to be back." I checked myself for injuries.

"We have been abducted by members of an unenlightened group."

"Gee. I thought they were just some kids having fun." I was checking my head with my hands.

"At least you have some wits about you. Many people would be dazed for several minutes after waking from a shock beam."

"Shock beam?"

"Shock beam guns freeze a person in their tracks and render them unconscious. They are only to be used by authorities. Enlightened persons have no need for them. I wonder how our abductors came by one. An agent would rather die than give up his weapon."

"What do you suppose these people want?"

"I do not know. Some factions of the unenlightened are criminals. They usually look for revenge, or are religiously motivated, meaning they belong to an old-world group that escaped enlightenment. These do not seem to be religious.

"I know of no reason for them to want revenge on you. Therefore, I assume they may be related to one of my past cases. Of course, there could be some motivation I am not aware of."

"What about ransom? That's what kidnappers of our time were often looking for."

"Ransom for currency wouldn't work in this time. All currency transfers are recorded in the world controllers, so authorities would find out who they were the instant they tried to collect credits.

"Twenty-nine years ago, some kidnappers tried to arrange a juggling of accounts, but they failed. They delayed identification by only two minutes. Since then, there have been six ransom attempts, and only one of them was for credits. The rest were for other reasons, and none have succeeded. That's why this current situation is so strange. It seems ludicrous for anyone to attempt something like this."

"Maybe they didn't take history in school."

I laughed, then immediately stopped as I noticed Henry didn't laugh. His face was blank.

After I stopped laughing, he smiled and said, "Perhaps you are right."

Our conversation was interrupted as two of the three people from the transport pod came into the room. The redheaded woman was now wearing a yellow outfit. The man wore two tone brown.

The redheaded woman and the man came over to me and helped me to my feet. Then the man bent over into my mid-section and lifted me onto his shoulder. Henry looked concerned as we left the room.

I was carried down a hallway to another room. The man stood me up and faced me away from him. The room appeared to be empty and the walls were bare. A screen covered the wall to my right.

He then shoved me onto a cushioned seat that appeared as I fell. I was able to upright myself.

The brunette had been waiting. She was wearing bright blue bottoms with a pale blue top. The three of them gathered around me.

The brunette spoke. "Where is your computer?"

So, that's what this was about. Somehow, they knew about Patricia.

I determined they would not find out from me. "What are you talking about?" I was hoping they didn't know enough detail to continue.

"You know what I'm talking about. We want access to your computer."

"Seriously, I don't know what you mean. What's a computer?"

"Mr. Gray. You will meet with significant injury if you continue to deny the existence of the computer you call Patricia."

She knew my name! Where did she get her information? How did she know about Patricia?

I began to fear the worst. Would they be able to get this information out of me? Did they have some way to do so? I continued to deny her existence, but they wouldn't buy it.

"We know as fact you are Gregory Allen Gray and you invented a computer that can see into the future. We are determined to have access to this computer. If you do not voluntarily tell us where it is, we will take strong measures to force it out of you. If necessary, we will use an enlightenment apparatus to make you one of us with the same goals we have. Do you want that? Do you want to live the rest of your life as one of us?"

"No, I wouldn't want that. I don't know what you are talking about. My name is Bruce Willis." It was what I came up with at the time.

Her look was stern. She turned to her comrades and gave a nod. They left the room. She glared at me for what seemed like the longest time.

Her comrades returned with Henry over the man's shoulder. They shoved him onto a cushion next to me, pointing the shock device toward him. "You are Henry, are you not?"

"Yes, I am."

"This is your charge, Mr. Gray, is it not?"

I tried to complain, but the redhead clamped a hand over my mouth. It hurt. She was stronger than she appeared.

Henry said, "Yes, he is Mr. Gray."

The brunette turned toward me. "Okay, Mr. Gray. Do you want to continue your charade?"

I didn't know what to do. I agreed I was indeed Gregory Allen Gray, but I didn't know anything about a computer.

She said, "Henry. Do you know anything regarding Mr. Gray's computer?"

"I do not. My orders are to accompany Mr. Gray wherever he wants to go, with a few exceptions. I was given little other information."

He didn't know anything about Patricia as far as I knew. Why was he being so cooperative? As if in explanation to my question, the brunette turned back to me.

"The enlightened always tell the truth, Mr. Gray. They never lie nor refuse to answer a question, unless commanded to do so by a superior. You, however, are lying. You will eventually tell us the truth. You can save yourself a lot of misery by telling us what we want to know."

I wished I hadn't lied about my name. I continued to deny Patricia's existence. Since Henry didn't know anything, he couldn't tell them otherwise.

They continued to question me for half an hour, resorting to threats of breaking my fingers. Then, suddenly, the brunette stalked out of the room and her comrades followed.

The women returned a few minutes later. The redhead was carrying a gray case. She flopped it onto a nearby table. She told the case to open and it did.

"Mr. Gray. You will tell us what we want to know, either voluntarily, or under the influence of this drug. This is a medication called Palscopolamento, a truth serum of sorts. It is a descendent of the drug your era knows as scopolamine. I'm sure Henry knows its effects. You will not be able to resist it and you will tell us everything we want to know. The drug will eventually destroy part of your brain. You will become a vegetable, unable to do or say anything after a few hours."

I looked at Henry. He nodded. No choice. I told them what they wanted to know. I gave them the location of the house.

"Is it true this computer can see into the future?" The redhead asked this question. I looked at Henry and then nodded.

The women were excited and anxious to go. They summoned the man they called Sampson. He was ordered to keep us in the room while they checked out the address. They left and Sampson locked us in the room.

They were gone about an hour. Suddenly, the two women stormed back into the room.

The brunette looked at me sternly and accusingly. "There was nothing there. Why did you lie again? You will not enjoy what the drug does to you! Where is the computer you call Patricia?"

Henry interrupted in a matter-of-fact voice. "He was telling the truth. He knows nothing more. My superiors told me this would happen. The computer must have destroyed itself to prevent you access."

They look dismayed. The brunette motioned the other two out of the room. They left.

I stared at Henry. Was it possible he knew about Patricia? Did she really destroy herself? She was supposed to exist for another two hundred and ten years! He, so very slightly, shook his head. I gathered I wasn't supposed to talk.

They have the room bugged, I thought. I decided to play along as if they did.

"Henry. Why did you tell me to tell them where Patricia is? I certainly didn't want her to self-destruct! I was hoping she would find another way."

"She must have known this would happen. The redhead said she could see the future. She sent a message to my superiors telling them this would happen. I didn't know who she was until the woman called her Patricia, so I couldn't tell our captors anything about a computer. I was truthful all the while.

"My superiors told me to give you a message if we were questioned about a female close to you. They told me nothing of a computer, only the name Patricia."

"Really? What's the message?"

"She wants you to know everything is going as it should. Do not mourn her death. She said you would remember she told you when she would die. She said to tell you she was truthful then, though you didn't believe her. That's a verbatim quote of her message."

Okay! Patricia wasn't destroyed! If she was truthful, then she would have two hundred and ten more years to survive.

I hid my excitement at this news. I suspected our captors were watching. I bowed my head as though in mourning, but I was smiling inside.

A few moments later, Sampson and the redhead returned. Now, the redhead was in command. "My name is Terra. You will construct a new computer for us. If you don't, your agent friend will die. You will be drugged and wind up nothing more than a vegetable. Do you agree?"

I looked at Henry, who nodded almost imperceptibly, and I nodded consent to their terms. "It may not turn out as Patricia did. We never discovered how she became able to see the future."

"Nevertheless, you shall try."

Terra nodded toward Sampson. Sampson approached and helped both of us to our feet. He then shoved us toward the opening to the room.

I wondered why nobody mentioned last names. In my time, if I introduced myself to someone, I would have included a last name.

We were led down a hallway to another room. This room was a laboratory of some kind. There was a bench top with two stools and various cabinets above and below. On the bench was a vocal interface.

Terra led the way and spoke into the interface. A moment later a ray of light emanated from one of the cabinets. Several computer components like those of my time slowly appeared on the bench. I recognized many of the components.

"Sit down and get to work."

I sat down and began assembling a computer as best I could from memory. I attempted to simulate the original circuitry making Patricia so special. I knew it would not work as our captors wanted, since Patricia and I tried it three times. We were unable to create a sister to Patricia. That mysterious electrical spark that occurred when I first hooked up her backup batteries must have been key to her development. We had been unable to duplicate the incident.

It was late, and I tired quickly. They made me try for two hours after I told them I was too tired to function properly. Eventually they took Henry and me back to the room where we first awakened. I slept hard. I was totally worn out.

The next day, I asked for some components Terra had not provided. It took another seven hours to complete the assembly.

Terra made me demonstrate the computer I built. I showed her how everything worked. She was a quick learner and asked many pertinent questions.

When we finished the training, Terra ordered us back to our room. We were left there for two hours.

We were sure they were monitoring us, so Henry and I kept our conversations light. I tried to end the situation, continuing with the pretense Patricia was dead.

"I can't duplicate Patricia. She and I tried together three times to develop a second computer with her capabilities. Since Patricia is gone, I don't know why they would keep us."

It didn't work. Another hour passed.

I asked if we could have some music. My wish was granted.

While the music was playing, I whispered and asked Henry if he had any idea how we could get out of this situation.

Henry whispered back.

"I do. I have been under orders, hoping to find out what others are involved. We need to get all three in the room at the same time."

"What would they do if I pretended to be sick?"

"I don't know. They might attempt some remedy of their own, or they might take you to a self-help medical station. They couldn't take you anywhere where authorities might get involved."

"Do you think they would all come in to check on me?"

"I doubt it. We need a better idea."

I thought for a moment. "I think I have an idea. Just go along with whatever I say."

I waited until the music slowed at the end of a song and then spoke out loud, "You know Patricia is okay, don't you?"

"You're kidding."

"No, the message you gave me told me she is alive. She told me she would live two hundred and ten years beyond this time. So, she must be alive. I don't know how she fooled our captors, though. I'm sure the message you were given was part of the ruse. She didn't want me to worry."

"Are you making this up?"

"Absolutely not. It's one hundred percent truth. I'm sure if we went to the house, Patricia would reveal herself to you and me."

Henry and I candidly discussed some of Patricia's abilities. It was ten minutes before the brunette and Sampson entered the room.

"The computer you assembled is of no use to us. Today's controllers are much better. You will accompany us to the house where Patricia is located."

"What are you talking about? Where is Terra?"

"We overheard your conversation. We know your computer did not self-destruct. I will pick Terra up along the way. Sampson will stay here with Henry."

She nodded to Sampson, who came toward me with cuffs. As he was binding my hands, I told her I wanted Henry to go with us. She denied the request.

I sat down, telling her I would refuse cooperation unless Henry went with us. She threatened to destroy him instead, pointing an item that looked like a Star Trek phaser at Henry.

I prayed she didn't want to hurt either of us. I persisted, telling her she couldn't threaten Henry if he weren't with us. She finally relented, much to my relief.

I asked a question as we left the room and started down the hall. "What is that weapon?"

"It's not a weapon. It's an old-style communicator. We use them to avoid detection by world controllers. I was bluffing."

I said under my breath, "Thank God."

She asked, "Why do you want Henry with us?"

"I don't want to be alone in this situation. I've never been in a situation like this before. I'm scared."

She looked at Sampson, laughing, "Definitely unenlightened!"

Sampson said, "No doubt!"

I said, "What's so strange about such feelings."

"Nothing, to us. The enlightened, though, have memories implanted giving them confidence in any situation. I suppose that might be good, but it's not real."

Henry said, "Of course, it's real. It's better for people to realize they don't have to generate unreasonable emotions in any situation. The more you are in control of negative emotions, the better you can function."

Sampson placed his shock beam gun to Henry's head. "Does this make you afraid?"

"No, it doesn't. I know you aren't going to use your weapon right now. If you did use the shock beam, I would wake up in half an hour. Why should I be afraid?" Sampson glared at him for a moment before lowering the weapon.

The brunette glared at Sampson. "We don't need these mind games."

Sampson looked crushed for a moment, then raised his head defiantly and walked on.

We left the building and entered the vehicle used when we were kidnapped. The brunette spoke the commands to take us to my house. The vehicle lifted into the air and headed off at a rapid pace.

I said, "Isn't this a city?"

Henry said, "Yes. It looks like Palmdale."

"Then why isn't there more traffic than I see?"

"Oh, that's right. In your time, people were always going somewhere and there were such things as traffic jams with your primary mode of transportation, land vehicles, were they not?"

Henry paused and I nodded.

"The people of your time traveled to offices to do their work. In this time, people do such work at home. There is no need to travel to meet with others when they can do it in their backyard. They can meet virtually face to face and work on projects together. They can touch each other and smile at each other.

"I would guess eighty percent of people today never need to leave their dwelling, unless they want to. They have food and other goods either delivered or fabricated right in their homes. They have backyards to provide entertainment and exercise."

"Don't they have slackers? Don't some people goof off instead of working?"

"The people have been enlightened. They know what they do is necessary for the good of all concerned. They know it is not in their interest to 'goof off', as you so quaintly say. It would not occur to them to do so. Besides, they have chosen their work. They are doing what they like to do."

The brunette spoke up angrily, "That's crap! They have been brainwashed to like their work."

"Not so." Henry said, "They truly pick their own work after trying many vocations. Do you not know of the work selection process?"

"All I know is what my father tried to get me to do. He wanted me to continue his work as a graphics artist. I hated giving commands to a controller all day. He constantly told me I'd learn to like it. I never did. I like being active and doing physical things. I loved playing soccer in the park playgrounds."

Henry seemed genuinely empathetic. "I'm disappointed that happened to you. If you were enlightened, you would have participated in work selection. You could have chosen your own profession. You could have been a Federation soccer player."

"I don't need your pity or your sarcasm!"

She clearly took Henry's comments to mean something other than intended.

I blinked my eyes in astonishment and wonder at this gross miscommunication. I'm sure I frowned. How could she have taken Henry's comments this way?

We rode in silence. I guessed Henry decided it was not possible to communicate with the brunette, and I certainly did not want to stir up any negative emotions. I watched the scenery.

We landed after a few minutes to pick up Terra. She had changed clothes and now wore a tan and brown outfit. She sat in the front since Sampson was in the third-row seat behind Henry and me. All three were together now, but I guessed it was not in a way Henry could act.

The vehicle finally descended into a wooded region, twisting its way through the intricate pattern of openings in the brush. I guessed Patricia not only allowed it but helped the vehicle's controller make its way through the maze. We touched down on a small, grown up lawn in front of my house.

I did not recognize it at first, although I had left there only a few days before. The house was covered in vines and other growth and it was hard to see it was a house. The lawn was much smaller than in my time, and the weeds grew to more than a foot high. It seemed apparent no one lived here.

How had Patricia accomplished all this?

The women took me in first, leaving Henry and Sampson in the vehicle. Sampson held the shock gun against Henry's back.

We entered the house and went down the hall to the lab. A layer of dust covered the floor. As we entered the lab, it appeared empty and smaller. Patricia had generated a holographic wall in front of her.

Terra was first to speak in a harsh tone, "Okay, Mr. Gray, where is your computer?"

"Gee. I don't know. It looks like she has been moved."

She gestured to the brunette who left the room. A few minutes later she returned with Sampson and Henry. "Now, Mr. Gray, if you do not tell us where Patricia is, we will injure Henry."

I looked at Henry. He nodded.

I said, "Patricia, please reveal yourself."

Our three captors watched in awe as the wall dissolved and Patricia appeared.

Henry made his move. He took advantage of the distraction to disarm Sampson. Then, much to my surprise, he snapped the cuffs on his hands, breaking them in two with little effort. He pulled me to one wall, then flung Sampson past the women and against the opposite wall.

The brunette was frozen with a look of shock. Terra began to get angry, yelling at Sampson, then held herself in check. She looked around at the brunette and then back at Henry who stood ready to defend himself, and me. Then, a look of realization and resignation came over her face. Henry relaxed and picked up the shock gun.

Patricia was the first to speak. "Hello Greg. I am glad to see things are in order."

I shook off my disbelief. "Hi, Patricia. I'm glad to see you. Henry. Terra. Meet Patricia."

"Great Hope Henry. Great Hope Terra. Great Hope Sampson. Great Hope, Shondell." Patricia displayed a knowledge beyond what transpired in her presence. I finally knew the brunette's name.

Henry responded first, "Great Hope, Patricia. I've heard a lot about you. I'm glad to meet you."

"And I, you, Henry. It's delightful to meet someone I might consider something of a peer."

I looked at Henry. What was Patricia talking about? How did Henry break the cuffs? What was going on?

Patricia spoke as if she knew what I was thinking. "Henry will explain everything to you in a few minutes, Greg. Right now, you and he need to confine the arms of the others."

As she talked, a beam emanated from her cabinet and two sets of cuffs appeared on the table.

Patricia spoke to me, "Greg, step over and hold your cuffs in front of me."

I moved over in front of Patricia. A different beam appeared. This beam was green and directed toward the cuffs on my wrists. They came loose and I caught them as they started to fall.

Henry picked up the other two cuff sets and approached the threesome. He bound Sampson first, then Terra. I handed him my cuffs and he used them on Shondell. He pulled the communicator off Shondell's waist. She glared at him.

"You are an android?"

"Hybrid."

Shondell was surprised. "I thought hybrids were science fiction."

"Very few know of our existence. We are a secret of the Federation of the Americas. Few know of us, and those that do are enlightened to keep the secret."

Henry looked in my direction. "You, Mr. Gray, may be the one exception to the rule. I will have to discuss it with my superiors."

He looked back at the threesome. "All of you will be enlightened. Don't worry, it doesn't hurt, and you will be much better for the experience."

They looked fearful and defeated. I almost felt sorry for them.

I'm not sure I agree with enlightenment. It has its pros and cons. It seems like good versus evil brainwashing to me. It was not my call to make, nor my place to interfere, so I remained quiet.

Henry turned toward me. "I am a hybrid. I have been an agent of the Federation of the Americas since I first chose a profession. My body was partially destroyed in an accident several years ago. They made new parts for me. It is identical to my original body, with much more physical power. It took more than two years for me to learn to control it, like learning to walk and talk again.

"At first, I was disgusted by the thought of mechanical parts. As time went on, I got used to the idea. Now, it feels like my real body. It's like the way people get used to false teeth and bridges."

"O-kay." I did not know how to respond to this information. "What are we gonna do now?"

Henry turned toward the three people on the other side of the room. "We are going to take these three to regional headquarters." He motioned for them to leave the room.

I hesitated for a moment, thinking I should stay for retrieval. I recalled my agreement with Patricia in my time was for me to stay here a week. It was now only three days. If I stayed, I wouldn't have anything to eat or drink for four days. I told Patricia I'd be back and followed the group out of the house. You can imagine my surprise to find the lawn freshly manicured, even where the pod we arrived in was parked.

I was also surprised to see Diva parked next to Terra's pod. I asked Henry why she was there.

"Diva is programmed to stay with me. She has been nearby all the time since we left the park. She monitors my brain waves. If I begin to get too far away, she follows at a discreet distance. As you know, Diva has access to the world controllers and probably to Patricia as well. Diva must have gotten instruction from her to come through the brush maze."

Henry ushered the threesome into their vehicle and told Diva to take control of it. Their pod closed and we climbed into Diva for the ride to headquarters. The trip took ten minutes.

We parked on the lawn behind the Federation of the Americas Northwest AM Regional Headquarters. A full color image announced the location as it displayed backgrounds and pictures of landscapes and people. We departed the transport pod.

Terra's pod was on the ground. It opened at Henry's command and he motioned the threesome out of the vehicle.

He explained to me, "This is where the Van Nuys airport was once located. Such smaller airports are no longer needed since transport pods can easily take you to the main airports and commercial air travel is rare compared to your time."

The two-story building covered an entire block. There didn't seem to be any security at the entrance. We walked through the wall and went inside.

We entered a forest pathway with blue sky and clouds overhead. As we proceeded, I noticed other paths leading left and right from our path. We turned at the fourth one on the left. We entered an office setting in a clearing in the forest.

A woman was sitting at a table, or was it a desk? It was a flat table, wide enough and low enough, to be a desk. It appeared to be suspended in midair.

The woman at the desk looked to be in her mid-forties, large framed, and about five foot one. Her black hair was curly and fell to her shoulder blades. She was wearing a tan form fitting top with brown pants.

Henry bid her great hope, calling her Stacy. She told us to wait to the right side of the room. We all moved to the indicated area and found seats that appeared as we approached.

It was a few moments before a man entered the room. He was broad shouldered, five foot ten, with curly brown hair and brown eyes. His face seemed weathered and he appeared to be fifty years old.

The form fitting style of the day was obviously not for him as he wore a dark blue loose top garment like an old Nehru jacket. He wore matching dark blue trousers that fit loosely, looking far too big for him. The entire ensemble seemed contrary to the styles I witnessed in this time.

He was followed by another man. He was taller and slimmer, and his outfit was more in style. His two-tone orange outfit was bright, almost fluorescent. He wore an orange cap reminiscent of a ball cap, but strangely different. The bill portion was short with multiple facets instead of being rounded, and the cap seemed to be form fitted to his head, coming down around his ears, but not over them.

The man in orange took charge of the three kidnappers and led them from the room. Terra looked back at me with what seemed like a strange mixture of anger and sorrow. Shondell's head was lowered. Sampson, with his head held high and his eyes lowered, seemed defiantly compliant, if that makes any sense.

The first man greeted me with an outstretched hand. "Great Hope Mr. Gray. I am Candor."

"Hi, Candor. You can call me Greg."

I shook his hand. His grip was light. His skin seemed tight, and a little rough. I remember thinking his obvious position seemed administrative, but his hands didn't indicate a soft job.

"Okay. Greg it is. That is more suitable for these times. No one has more than one name anymore." Candor smiled. "Identity these days is confirmed by controllers sensing several individual traits in our brain waves, voices, bodily scents, eyes, breathing patterns, and fingerprints. It is impossible to fool them once they have your data.

"If you have ever been in contact with a controller and your identity confirmed, you are in the world record. For most of us, it happens at birth and updates as we develop into adults. It happened for you when you met Diva. We have always possessed your voice, fingerprint, and eye patterns, and now she has all your other data as well."

"What's gonna happen to Terra and the others? How did they get past the age of enlightenment? Didn't your controllers know about them?"

Candor explained it all in a monotone voice reminiscent of Patricia. "Twenty years ago, there were some problems with the world controllers, despite multiple redundant systems. I am not at liberty to go into detail regarding the incident.

"Several hundred people were listed as enlightened when they, in fact, did not get enlightened. Most are discovered as they display unenlightened characteristics in public. A few have learned to purposely hide themselves from discovery.

"When they make a mistake, we find them. They are then enlightened and truly fit in with today's society. Your kidnappers will find enlightenment to be a valuable experience. It will prepare them for a much better life."

"How do you know about me—and Patricia?"

I looked intently into Candor's eyes as I asked the question. I wanted to see if he was as candid about this as he seemed to be about everything else. He was. Then I remembered Terra said enlightened people always tell the truth.

"I have read part of the book you will write when you get back to your time. Patricia has not allowed me to read it all—yet."

"What book? I've never written a book in my life. Why would I start now?"

Candor smiled as he answered.

"I imagine it will be due to your unique experience during this time trip of yours. It is an adventure no one before or since has accomplished.

"You are the one man in history that has achieved time travel. That is why you will author a book. No one in your time will believe it. No one in our time will be allowed to read it until you are back to your own time. They will think it was written by someone in this decade, due to detail you provide. Patricia arranged it that way. She said it was in the best interest of the world."

I now knew he had contact with Patricia. "Sounds like you and Patricia have spoken."

"Not exactly. She has contacted me in written messages. She allowed me to read part of your book in such a message. I do not know where she is located. Diva and Henry are forbidden to divulge such information. I know each would die, rather than do so. The three that abducted you will have similar instruction. They will know it to be in their best interest to die, rather than divulge that information."

"Enlightenment is that strong?"

"Absolutely. The process implants real memories. If you have an experience that tells you it's in your best interest to defend or protect, do you not do so?"

"Yes. I did so when we were kidnapped, until Henry indicated I should do otherwise. What if these people get such an indication?"

"It will not happen. Patricia has informed me so." Candor said it matter-of-factly. "You will use some falsehoods in your book. No one will be able to discover Patricia's location."

"The names have been changed to protect the innocent." I remembered the phrase from an old Dragnet show I saw on television.

Would I write such a book? I supposed it might be possible, but it wasn't something I considered before. I guessed I would do it, since it was written.

Does that make sense? I wondered.

"Thank you, Candor. That makes me feel a lot better."

Knowing the future in some cases is reassuring. Can you imagine how I might feel if I thought divulging Patricia's location to those three would eventually create enormous problems for the entire world? If something you told Adolf Hitler caused him to do what he did, how would you feel? I felt relieved to know my actions would not create havoc in the world.

I realized I was operating entirely under a type of protection, since Patricia knew what would happen. It gave me confidence to know I would be getting back to my own time. There were a couple of times during this adventure when I was uncertain.

As Henry and I left the building, he asked what I wanted to do now.

"Is it okay to go to Los Angeles now?"

"We're already there, at least in the upper valley. I have been given new instruction from Candor. You are free to go wherever you want."

I wanted to see the beaches, but soon discovered they weren't there.

Patricia – 100 Years into the Future

Freedom

Between a meteor strike, earthquakes, the rising ocean, and erosion, the beaches of my time suffered extinction. Entire cities disappeared in the process. As Diva hovered above, I watched waves break against hills and cliffs far from where the beaches used to be. I was shocked to see the changes along the ocean front.

The ocean was much higher than in my time. Some of the broken ice in the polar cap drifted south and melted after the asteroid impact. Land erosion helped increase water levels. While I could recognize some of the canyon and hill areas, the region was not nearly what I knew. Manhattan Beach, the city I lived in, was gone. Palos Verdes rose out of the water as an island.

The beaches and many of the cities I knew were gone. Parts of the Pacific Coast Highway were gone without a trace. Malibu beach was gone. Long Beach harbor was not there. Marina Del Rey did not exist. Much of Hollywood was gone with only hills remaining as islands. What I knew as North Hollywood had survived.

I said, "What happened? Did many people die in the process?"

"Yes. Some did. However, it's not like it happened suddenly, as it may seem to you right now. It has occurred over many years.

"It began in August of 2048 with a tsunami created by an asteroid impacting the ocean between here and Hawaii. The primary wave was twenty-three meters high. The run-up was four hundred meters—more than thirteen hundred feet in terms you know. Many people drowned. Many buildings were damaged, and some washed away.

"It is estimated the incident caused a series of earthquakes near a place known as Chino Hills. The first few were relatively minor being only magnitude 5.3 to 5.4 on the Richter Scale. These quakes shook the entire LA region and were felt eighty kilometers away but caused insignificant damage.

"It was determined years later those quakes seriously disturbed a fault near the Kenneth Hahn Recreation Area at Baldwin Hills. Until then, the area generated quakes but none over 2.0 in magnitude, which, as I'm sure you know, is barely felt.

"In December of 2048, there was a 7.3 magnitude quake centered there. A 7.3 magnitude quake is much stronger than a 5.4 since the Richter Scale is not a linear scale. That quake opened a fissure running from the north side of Santa Monica near Palisades Park to Ladera Heights and then down through parts of Inglewood. It destroyed many buildings and roadways.

"A second 6.6 quake the following week opened a fissure from Inglewood further south to Gardena. A third quake three weeks later, magnitude 7.4, opened the rift down to Alamitos Bay. It created a dozen other fissures that spread inland to the hills and washed soil into the ocean.

"The fissures are nine kilometers deep in places. As the ocean poured in, steam poured out creating low lying clouds so laden with moisture they were unable to leave the basin. They poured out rain at the base of the surrounding hills.

"The situation caused mud slides into the crevices and washed soil out to the ocean. The cities in the Los Angeles basin were devastated and in ruin. Many people died during those quakes and their aftermath. Aftershocks as high as magnitude 5.9 led to more destruction. Much of the basin was divided as fissure after fissure opened to the sea. The whole area was in a state of destruction and turmoil.

"The basin was evacuated during the weeks after the third quake. It took time to get to some of the people, despite efforts of the California National Guard and assistance from the military.

"Many survived on food and supplies dropped into larger land areas. Thousands and thousands died. Some people in smaller sized land areas fended for themselves for weeks. The result was nearly three fourths of the Los Angeles basin was lost to the sea and more than four million people died in the process."

Wow! What a tale! I remembered all the warnings in the latter part of the twentieth century. Earthquakes were part of life in sunny California. Doomsday predictions were, too. I would try to warn them, but I was sure people would not believe me. It finally happened. I was glad I moved from the area.

I thanked Henry for the information, and we headed toward Palmdale. I was wondering where I would sleep. Should I get some food and take it to the house? It seemed a promising idea until I remembered no one lived in the house for twelve years. I would have to clean before I could consider staying there.

Henry chose that moment to let me know I would be staying with him. "You will need a place to stay tonight. I have been instructed to take you to my residence. I live in the mountains west of Palmdale, which is why I was assigned to you. I am the closest agent to your house. We will arrive shortly. Is there anything we need to do before we get there?"

"Well, I am getting hungry. We haven't eaten since our captors gave us breakfast this morning."

"That is correct. I have a food station at my residence. We will eat as soon as we arrive."

We were now flying over the mountains past the San Fernando Valley. It was a different view from above. We passed over a canyon. I could see what I knew as Lake Palmdale off to the right although it was larger than I remembered. Diva turned away from it, heading up a valley to the left and descending to 150 feet off the ground. Below us was an unfamiliar waterway. We didn't go far.

Diva suddenly turned toward the middle of the 200-foot high cliff on my side of the transport, scaring me half to death. Diva passed through the side of the mountain and stopped suddenly in a cave, descending to a stony surface. I still had my arms up to protect my face. Henry's residence was built right into the side of the mountain and not detectable by me.

Henry laughed as we exited the pod, "I pray that didn't scare you too much. Dinah, my dwelling controller, projects an image so the entrance looks like the rest of the mountain side. Diva, of course, knows where to enter. I forgot to inform you."

The facility was impressive. We appeared to be in an entirely closed cave until Henry strode toward a certain formation and went right through the rock wall. I followed him inside.

We entered a scenic area of mountains and streams with wooded areas and waterfalls complete with sounds including the water falling and birds singing. We appeared to be in a clearing near a pool of water fed by a waterfall. It was certainly a relaxing place. I pivoted around in absolute wonder at the beauty of this place.

Henry invited me to take a seat. I didn't see a seat to take, only a round, discolored area on the ground in front of me. As I moved toward the area, a cushioned surface appeared in front of me. I sat and the soft cushion conformed to my body.

Henry sat four feet away facing me. A flat surface at a suitable height rose between us. A vocal interface rose from the middle of the table. Our seats turned and slid us forward to the right distance facing each other across the table.

I ordered the same meal I ordered at the food station I visited on my first day in the future. Henry ordered something entirely different. His meal looked like a large mound of chocolate ice cream and he ate eagerly.

I said, "What is that?"

"We call it kawbry. It's delicious. Would you like to taste it?"

He ordered another spork and offered me a spoonful of the semi-solid substance. I can only describe the taste as a cross between a semi-sweet chili and cranberry sauce. As gross as it may sound, it was delicious. I finished my meal and ordered a small dish of kawbry for myself. Having gone eight hours without eating, I was very hungry.

Henry suggested we sleep. He led me through a tree and showed me a sleeping surface next to a small waterfall. As comfortable as the area and sleeping surface was, I tossed and turned all night. I dreamed. I awoke. I dreamed again. I awoke. I dreamed again. I was finally sleeping peacefully when Henry shook me awake.

"It's time to get up. We will go to the office this morning. I'm anxious to hear what our captors say about why they wanted your computer."

I struggled to my feet, half asleep and groggy. Henry led me to a tree in the corner, walking through it into another clearing situated against a rock cliff. He showed me how to use modern facilities for grooming. He instructed me to face toward a specific section of the cliff. It became a mirror as I did. A curved pad came out of the cliff wall and Henry told me to put my forehead against it.

Henry instructed a vocal interface I could not see. "Straight brush to the sides, part left side."

I felt my hair brush forward and then to each side from a part on the left side of my head. It seemed miraculous.

I exclaimed involuntarily. "Wow. That was fast!"

"I understand that people of your time used something call a comb."

"Yes. Some use a brush."

"Sounds terribly time consuming."

"By this standard, I guess it is!"

I looked in the mirror at three days of beard growth and told Henry I could use a shave. He gave an instruction to remove the hair on my face below the centerline of my eyes. I saw a light beam come toward my face and felt something happen. It was over in less than five seconds.

I felt my face. It was clean shaven, and my skin felt smoother than ever. As I looked in the mirror, I noticed a small pimple was no longer there.

I asked Henry how it worked.

He replied, "The hair removal process smooths the skin and can remove minor imperfections. It follows with a conditioning that smooths the skin, filling in pores and imperfections. We take it for granted, but I suppose it's strange to you."

It was. Cleaning my teeth was equally amazing and expedient. No brushing included. I normally spent at least ten minutes in the bathroom at home. We were there less than three minutes and I was perfectly groomed.

"How does it work?" I asked.

"I've been instructed not to give you too much information, especially regarding how things work. I was informed that it is not in the best interest of the world for you to know such information."

Ugh!

We sat down for breakfast. I asked, "Is French toast available?"

"There are several variations. Do you know what you want?"

"Something with nutmeg and vanilla."

He tried, but there was nothing on the menu like I described. He asked the interface for a menu of French toast variations. The interface projected a list complete with images. I was stunned by the number of variations and stopped counting at sixty-three.

I found an item that sounded like what I wanted. A plate with two light brown six-inch squares 1-inch thick was served. It was tasty, though mysteriously different from what I usually fixed at home. Henry ate a bowl of something that looked like grits. He called it polenta.

As we ate, I asked Henry to tell me more about hybrids.

He said, "A hybrid is a person with some mechanical body parts. In my case, I have mechanical legs, arms, and three ribs on my right side. My heart, my kidneys, a portion of my sinuses, and the eye on my left side have been replaced. There are some people that have almost entirely new bodies."

"That sounds mostly new to me. I don't know how I would accept such a thing for myself."

"My accident was the result of an infrasonic blast when two unenlightened criminals tried to destroy a sonic dust chamber. The initial blast hit me on my left side. It knocked me over a hillside into a waterway. Automatic safety systems shut down the sonic blaster. Softer organs on the left side of my body were damaged. I landed in the low-level waterway on my right side damaging my right hip, ribs, and shoulder. Lyla, my old transport pod, immediately notified medical staff. I could have died.

"The unenlightened pair did not know what they were doing. They were unaware of the potential danger. They died in the blast. I understand their insides were transformed into an amorphous jelly. Their bodies were skin and bones with a sticky liquid oozing from various openings."

I gagged. "Henry, we're eating!"

He laughed. "Oh. Did that information cause you a challenge? Perhaps we need to strengthen your fortitude?"

"Yeah. And then we need to work on your etiquette."

We laughed.

Henry got up and said, "It's time to go."

I followed him to the exit, looking over my shoulder to observe the table clean itself and disappear into the ground floor of the clearing. Once again, I wondered how it all worked.

Diva turned around after we left her. As we stepped into the vehicle, the cave wall in front of us appeared to open to the sky. Diva rose from the surface and we zipped out, turning left as we cleared the opening.

It was a seven-minute trip to the headquarters building in the valley. I was quietly enthralled by the scenery as we traveled. Everything was so familiar yet distinctly different from what I saw in my time. The sagebrush covering the hills in 2008 was replaced by trees, brush, grass, and buildings on most hillsides.

As we entered the headquarters building and started down the pathway through the forest, a woman dressed in tight fitting black and gray attire was coming our way. She was ten feet from us when Henry spoke to her.

"Great Hope!"

"Great Hope to you, Henry. Who's your charge?"

We stopped and Henry introduced me to Chandra, a colleague. She was five foot six with shoulder length chestnut hair and a decorative comb pulling the hair back on each side. She was incredibly attractive, and I made such an observation.

"Wow. You are pretty."

She blushed. "Thank you, Greg. You are attractive as well."

She paused, then smiled at Henry.

"Great hope on your life journey."

"Great hope for your life journey."

She went on her way. We watched as she left the building. Henry then jerked his head toward the office, indicating we needed to continue.

He said, "That's the most conversation we ever had. I wasn't sure she was human."

"Pardon?"

"Some agents are androids. I thought she was one. An android would not have blushed, though. She's human after all. That's interesting."

We continued in silence as Henry appeared to be deep in thought. We entered the pathway into the office we were in the day before. I was surprised to see Candor waiting on us.

Candor greeted us, "Great hope this morning."

Henry said, "Great hope."

I remained silent.

Candor faced me. "Great hope to you as well."

"May I assume that is like 'good morning' in my time?"

"Uh. I guess it may be. I haven't heard that exact expression, though."

"Good morning to you, too."

They both laughed.

Candor said, "The three people you brought in yesterday have undergone partial enlightenment. They need nine more days for completion, but they are enlightened enough to answer some questions."

Candor turned his head and spoke to someone or something I couldn't see. It wasn't long before the man in orange brought Terra, Shondell, and Sampson into the room. We all sat down in a circular arrangement and a round table appeared between us. The three of them faced us. The man in orange remained standing behind them.

Candor spoke first, "How are you all today?"

Terra responded, "We all have great hope."

The others nodded in agreement.

"Did you sleep well?"

Terra said, "Yes, we slept very well. We want to thank you for bringing us in for enlightenment. We are apologetic for the actions we took in the past. We were wrong to have kidnapped Henry and Mr. Gray."

"Can you tell us why you wanted Mr. Gray's computer?"

Shondell responded this time. "We thought we could investigate the future and avoid capture. Additionally, we believed the ability to see the future would be helpful many other ways."

"Understandable. For someone who is not enlightened, that could be a powerful resource. Can you tell me if there are others working with you?"

I hadn't considered that. It meant I could still be in danger. My fears were confirmed.

Sampson spoke this time. "Yes. There are others we relate to. We do not know who they are. Our orders came through the old communicator Henry took from us."

Terra added, "We are part of a larger organization. We work together in groups of three. There will be others come after Mr. Gray's computer since we did not report yesterday.

"We understand our actions were not in the best interest of society. However, we do not know enough to help you find the others. We only know the name Appleton and we are certain it is not a real name. We don't know if anyone knows all the groups involved, or how many there are."

"How do they contact you? We have tried to communicate on that frequency and do not get an answer."

"We do not respond unless we hear the code word. The code word changes. Each time we communicate, a new code word is given for the next communication."

Wow! Enlightenment must work well. I could not imagine a criminal in my time responding like this.

"Do you have any idea how soon they might attempt to find Mr. Gray?"

Shondell answered, "No, sir. We do not. We know it will be soon. We know that Mr. Gray is scheduled to go back to his own time in four days. Today was a deadline set for us to find his computer. We were instructed to be cordial with him, but to do whatever necessary to carry out our orders."

Terra spoke up, "There is another thing you may find helpful. We gave our contact the coordinates Mr. Gray gave us the day we were unable to find his computer."

Uh. Oh. I felt alarmed. That was a scary thought for me. Then I remembered Patricia knew, and everything would be okay. I relaxed again.

Terra continued, "We reported finding nothing there but brushy woods. We thought Mr. Gray lied to us."

"What is the next code word for communicating?"

"Sponge."

Candor stood up and said, "Very well. You may return to your enlightenment chambers."

Shondell commented as she rose to her feet, "We are anxious to do so. We feel so relieved of many burdens and look forward to learning everything."

The three followed the man in orange from the room.

Candor sat back down facing Henry. "Henry, it looks like we may have work to do. Protect Mr. Gray and his computer at all cost. Do you concur?"

"Yes, I concur."

Henry stood up. He indicated I should remain there. He and Candor left the room.

I was lost in thought. What was I doing here? This should have been a simple expedition and exploration. I didn't expect to be involved with anyone else when I made the jump. Why was all this happening?

They were gone about five minutes. Henry and Candor returned with smiles on their faces.

Candor spoke, "We attempted to communicate with the new code word but got no answer. We have concluded you should enjoy your stay in our time. Henry will continue to escort you wherever you would like to go. He will act to ensure your safety as well."

As Candor left the room, we departed the same way we came in. Did they have a plan? Did Patricia tell them to do this? Was I in danger?

Walking down the hall, I asked Henry, "Am I in danger?"

"You will be fine. Candor assured me you will get back to your own time without injury. He was informed by Patricia. I have been assured all is happening as it should. You might consider what you'd like to do now."

"Okay." Then, slowly shaking my head, "I'm glad Patricia knows because I sure don't."

Henry smiled.

As we walked on, I wondered what I would like to do. I had seen so much, and things were so different than I could have imagined.

My mind was racing as we stepped into Diva. I thought mankind would be so much further evolved than this. I guessed the futuristic movies carried things a little too far. Teleportation was supposed to be a reality by now. Space travel should have been so much further along. What happened to warp drives and wormholes?

I was a little disappointed. I asked Henry about it as Diva rose into the air.

Henry smiled, "Yes, you undoubtedly would have such expectations. I have been briefed and studied some of those stories. They are fantasy, you know. The best and most expedient explanation is that people relaxed. They got involved in their games and fantasies for a lot of years.

"They quit moving forward in many ways. In 2062, a great income equalization experiment was mandated by Fredrick Grandi, who was Viceroy of North America at the time. His staff had formulated a plan whereby all people could have equal income and equal opportunity."

I interrupted him. "Viceroy of North America?"

"Oh, I suppose you would have questions. A little history is in order. After the Third World War destroyed . . ."

"Third World War?"

"Oh. It hadn't happened in your time? Oh, right. I'll have to back up further.

"In the year 2041, most of the world had grown extremely tired of various terrorist organizations exploiting young people to carry out special missions. It began with Muslim Jihadists secretly forming various groups throughout the world. Jihadists believed they had a mission to kill those people they called infidels. Infidels were people who did not believe as these radicals believed.

"You are from the year 2008 in the land called the United States of America. You may recognize the names of Christian radicals such as Jim Jones and David Koresh. Do you know of them?"

"Yes, I think both, and most of their followers died for their causes, didn't they? I know something about Jihadists after 911."

"Yes. That happened in 2001, didn't it?"

"True. Everyone learned about Jihadists and suicide bombers after that."

"Right. Jihadist groups had followers dying for their cause. Their leaders created a hierarchy so there was always someone ready to take over when the publicized leader died. Primary leaders allowed lower level commanders to represent themselves as group leaders. World governments sought out those publicized leaders and killed or captured them. They were replaced almost instantly.

"These leaders trained the young and impressionable to carry out suicide missions. The youngsters knew little but what these leaders taught them. The young people would kill as many infidels as they could and often be killed, either by authorities or by blowing themselves up. This was supposed to win them a wonderful place in an afterlife paradise.

"The real leaders, of course, were never in danger. They convinced others to do the dirty work for them.

"By the year 2041, there was so much killing around the world that most countries determined there was a need to wipe out the threats. They created a worldwide governing body from what was originally the United Nations.

"This included all the Muslim countries who joined because their religion was being misrepresented by the Jihadists. It was much the same as Jim Jones, David Koresh, and the Westboro Baptist Church misrepresented Christianity. The new body was named The Nations of Peace.

"Each country sent one representative to this body. The representatives elected a leader to facilitate their meetings. Most countries were teaching English to schoolchildren by then, primarily due to tourism and worldwide news reports. English was declared to be the new world language. The newly formed organization unanimously declared war on the many Jihadist groups developed by then.

"It was the beginning of World War Three and was the last war fought on this planet. Jihadist leaders and their followers were sought out around the world. They were either killed or deported from each country to an isolated place in the Sahara Desert. A huge detention center was built. Food and water were provided by the Nations of Peace.

"There was an attempt to educate them. It failed miserably. It is difficult to change a person's mind. It's been said that a man convinced against his will is of the same opinion still.

"The former leaders within the detention center fought among themselves. They tried to organize and break out, but their efforts failed.

"In September of 2045, one warfighting team obtained control of a nuclear missile in what was known as Russia.

They managed to fire the missile and guide it to the encampment. The event wiped out one point six million Jihadists, plus their guards.

"The fallout from the explosion spread across much of northern Africa and the Middle East killing many people and sickening many more. It was a sad day for much of the world. Like Hiroshima and Nagasaki, the event led to ending the war."

I interrupted, "Wow. I find it interesting that happened one hundred years after World War Two."

"Yes. The timing is intriguing. There were a few Jihadist leaders left in various places around the world, but their influence was broken. Some tried to form a new caliphate. There was always someone who reported to authorities. By then, everyone was onboard with preemptive strikes because war had been declared worldwide. Each group was wiped out before they could get fully organized.

"The death toll was calculated from all the suicide missions and war kills. All told, more than seventy million people lost their lives. It was one of the worst times in the history of mankind.

"Then they determined there were too many individual countries. It resulted in far too many differences and radical ideas. The Nations of Peace decided there needed to be fewer governing bodies. After more than a decade of conversations, it was determined each continent should be independent, leading to six separate entities in the world. Since people were not living in Antarctica, it had no representative. Each continent elected a Viceroy, who was a representative with the Nations of Peace, which determined policy for the entire world.

"Technology developed to the point where most people could access a food station. Most labor was being done by machines. People had little need to do any physical labor.

"In 2062 the Viceroy of North America, Fredrick Grandi, tried his experiment with income equality. Credits were developed and money was no longer used. Everyone was stripped of their fortunes and an equal income plan was instituted. It backfired.

"Everyone received the same compensation for their work. Eventually, few people would work on anything beyond their official duties. Jobs usually done by one or two people now required as many as eleven or twelve, sometimes more.

"People had little incentive to do well since it made no difference in their compensation. People's free time was taken up with game playing and recreation. Some people played on controllers so much that their leg muscles atrophied. Society in North America became stagnant for years.

"It was during this time the population exploded. Hedonist behavior abounded. People were getting together, and women were getting pregnant every year. Some couples had as many as eight children. Each child received equal compensation from the North American controller, so the larger the family, the more credits they received. It was the only way to increase income.

"After seven years the Viceroy and his staff reversed the equal income experiment. Their secret agenda became seeing how long it would take for income levels to return to previous levels. They were interested to see if those of lower income would find ways to rise above where they were previously. Some did, some didn't.

"This was prior to the current world order. The Americas were combined in 2071 along with many other countries. This became the Federation of the Americas.

"Jihadism was born again among some regions in northern Africa. To combat it, a man named Raheesh Inabi invented enlightenment technology. He brought his invention to the attention of The Nations of Peace in the year 2073. They unanimously determined it to be good for everyone. Together, and over many months, they decided on some basic tenets to be followed by every nation.

"Each Viceroy worked with their staff to determine the best programming for their people and submitted it to The Nations of Peace for approval. They decreed everyone should undergo the process. They decreed all couples would have no more than two children. Since controllers could identify people, it was decreed no more than one name was necessary.

"We are now being enlightened and know it is not in the best interest of the world to waste away our time on narcissistic activity. Remediation treatments are undergone once a month, so we are constantly aware of current technology and new challenges.

"We take time for recreation because we know it is necessary for our well-being. The time taken for such activity is limited to two hours, twice a day. The rest of our time is used to take care of our well-being, learn, and develop within our chosen field. Things are moving forward now. It's a slow pace compared to what you must have seen in your lifetime, but at least it is forward motion now."

I said, "Wow. What a story. I hate that so many people lost their lives. It seems to have worked out, though."

"Yes. Have you considered what you would like to do now?"

I had been involved in Henry's history. I looked outside. Diva was drifting south, and I was fascinated by the view. The coast I knew was no longer the same.

Patricia – 100 Years into the Future

Las Vegas

I was lost in thought for a few minutes as we floated above the coastline. I noticed Palos Verdes rising from the waters. There were hills rising here and there. I could see what was left of many buildings. I noticed a major fissure going through what I knew as Redondo Beach. It extended well out into the ocean. I could see Catalina Island off in the distance.

"Does Las Vegas still exist?" I asked.

"Yes, it does. Would you like to visit there? It's early and would only take Diva fifty minutes to arrive there."

"Only fifty minutes? That's more than 200 miles!"

Diva spoke, "Exactly 243.21 miles to city center. I can travel at two hundred sixty miles per hour. We can be there in fifty-six minutes. Shall I proceed?"

I looked at Henry. He shrugged, nodding his head to one side. "It is quite different than it was in your time. Going there can cost you credits if you do anything more than sightseeing."

"Diva, how many credits do I have in my account?"

"Twenty-eight million, two hundred thousand, three hundred and sixty four Americas credits. You are one of the top five thousand affluent people in the world."

What! How could that be?

Henry whistled, "Wow! And you've only been here for a few days."

He began laughing. I joined in with him.

"I think Patricia has been keeping my accounts. How much does a hamburger cost these days?"

Henry was puzzled. "What is a hamburger?"

"It is a popular sandwich in my time. It consists of ground beef in patty form topped with condiments such as catsup, mustard, or pickles."

"What is ground beef?"

"Don't you have cows? Beef is the meaty part of a cow."

"Oh yes, cows. I think some of the Mongolian States have cows. Don't they, Diva?"

"Yes, Henry, they do. There are approximately ten thousand cows in the Manitoban States. They use them to provide cargo transportation in rural areas."

I said, "Really? In my time, donkeys were used for cargo transportation in rural areas."

Henry responded, "What is a donkey? Oh, I remember from historical training. They are extinct now. They were infected with Beckwith Disease during the 2060s. The disease affected horses, zebras and donkeys. Those species were wiped out."

Wow. I wondered if other species of animals were extinct.

Diva spoke, "There have been sixteen species of animals go extinct in the last hundred years."

It was as if she had read my mind. I then realized she had read this book. She would know what I was thinking.

I said, "Okay. Let's see how Vegas has changed."

Henry said, "Diva, take us to Las Vegas."

Diva rose higher in the sky and changed direction. We made the trip mostly in silence and occasional small talk. As we glided past hills, valleys, cities and towns, I was enraptured by the sights. I was amazed that there seemed to be no desert areas. Everything appeared lush and green. There were rounders everywhere.

When Las Vegas was finally in sight, I was astonished. It was so much larger than in my time. It stretched southward and northward far more than in my time. What I knew as the town of Jean was at the southern border and the northeastern section now bordered the area I knew as the Moapa River Indian Reservation. The northwestern section had grown up to include Indian Springs.

Buildings were not as high as I remembered and there were many more of them. Most of the taller buildings were round with woods in the center and took up an entire rounder. The rounders were large, and grassy commonways separated them. Smaller buildings were only one or two stories. Henry advised most of those were residential.

Construction was far different than in my time. The taller buildings were built in tiers. Each tier was three stories high. There were some as many as five tiers high with each tier a little smaller than the previous one. I saw no lighted signs. In fact, I saw no signs at all.

"Why are there no signs?" I asked.

Diva said, "All transport pods have information on each of the vacation stations. There is no need for signs or all the lights you knew."

When I commented about the tiered buildings, Henry explained, "Do you remember the erector we saw constructing the playground at the park?"

"Yes."

"Erectors are used to create structures. While structures can be created next to another to provide width and length, the erectors can only create up to twelve meters in height. Designers of these buildings had a choice. They could design larger erectors, an impractical task due to Glaser beam dispersion causing the beam to be ineffective and error prone after a certain distance, or design buildings that could be built using erectors already in use.

"The taller buildings, then, are built in sections, or tiers, eleven meters high. Each tier provides support for the erector to create the next higher tier. Thus, the space on both sides of each tier. The space is wide enough to be used for parking, so it is practical as well."

"Are these casinos?"

"Not as you may know them. All but the first floor are temporary living quarters. In your time, they would have been called hotels."

"That fits with my time. Casinos were built with hotel rooms above. What happened to them? I don't see the Stratosphere either."

"Jihadists are primarily responsible for their destruction. These buildings do not have casinos on the first floor. People can play all such games in their backyards. The first floor of these stations consists of show rooms. You would know such places as theaters.

"You see, the only thing we cannot duplicate in our playgrounds is live shows. We can create holoshows, but they are predictable since we specify or program them. Live shows, therefore, are sought after. Some can be seen with Holovision, but many people desire to be in a live audience. All the live shows in vacation resorts are kept private. They are not available to be seen anywhere else.

"Las Vegas is the only place in the Northwestern Region that has live shows. There is New York in the Northeastern Region, Rio de Janeiro in the Southeastern Region, Lima in the Southwestern Region, Perth in Western Australian Region, Brisbane in Eastern Australia Region, Kendari in the Indonesia Region, Paris in the European Region, Stockholm in the Scandinavian Region, and Reykjavik in the Greenland-Iceland Region.

"Many people come to Las Vegas each year. It is a resort place and these buildings are known as vacation resorts. Most visitors stay at least two weeks."

Diva began descending and asked Henry where we wished to finish the trip. Henry responded that the Diamond Live Plaza would be fine.

"Diva, please provide some town history for Mr. Gray."

"Agreed. From what date do you wish to know, Greg?"

I was watching the view below and listening intently to Henry's description. I didn't know where to start. I stretched my words as I thought about it.

"O-ka-y, Di-v-a, let's start with World War Three. It's not hard to imagine how the town would be until then. Oh, and keep it brief. I don't need a lot of detail. Just give me the highlights, please."

"Agreed. In February of 2041, war was declared against Jihadist terrorists. That began World War Three.

"Prior to that time, Las Vegas was one of several favorite targets for terrorists. There were people in the casinos and on the streets, so suicide bombers and snipers could kill and injure many people at one time. Casinos were severely damaged due to the explosions. The town eventually shut down to avoid being targeted. Many casino employees were out of work and joined the war effort.

"The internet had developed to very-near-real-time and available everywhere. In April of 2043, the Nations of Peace declared it legal, and all gambling occurred online. This was done to help keep people from gathering where terrorists could strike.

"Poker players preferred to play the game in person. This was due to the desire to be able to read opponents for tells. Tells are small indications given by eye movement, facial twitches, and gestures that could let a person know if their opponent has a good hand or trying to bluff. Bluffing means they are betting and hoping they don't get called, letting them win a hand by default.

"As the war was ending, the town began rebuilding. Early versions of today's erectors were used, keeping the buildings low, and the city was laid out in rounders. Early rounder design had central amenities like swimming pools, tennis courts, golf facilities, and other attractions for use by casino guests.

"The town was open for business again in early December of 2045. It was a slow start. Many people had been involved in the war effort and were just getting back to work. Few had resources available for travel and entertainment.

"So, as the city was rebuilt, concentration was on live shows and poker games. Poker was played in casinos for several years. Other games could be played anywhere, online while in your room, or while sitting in a garden or restaurant. There was no need for the expensive machines used previously."

By this time, we were positioned in a ground level parking area at one of the tall buildings. I asked Diva to continue with history and we waited.

"After the coastal disasters, more than four million people moved to the area. This prompted much residential expansion. The city was growing and alive once again.

"By 2050, the utilities serving Las Vegas were stretched to their limits. The water level in Lake Mead was getting lower each year despite record rainfalls and snow melts in the mountainous regions feeding the Colorado River. Grand Lake and Lake Granby in Colorado, and other lakes lowered their water levels to help maintain levels in Lake Mead. Las Vegas and Clark County officials began refusing new residents.

"Then something amazing happened. Weather patterns changed. Suddenly there were moisture laden clouds coming from the Pacific Ocean."

I said, "What caused that?"

"Scientists theorize the asteroid crash in 2048 had much to do with the changes. Ocean water was vaporized when the asteroid entered the sea and it drifted eastward with the winds. Some vaporization continues due to a warmer ocean. Higher water levels were due to ice melts and higher temperatures in the northern Pacific Ocean.

"Ozone loss was created in 2049 by secret experiments that I cannot detail for you. These were conducted by order of the Nations of Peace north of the equator in the middle of the

Pacific Ocean. The sun in that area of the world has been dangerously hot since then.

"The theory is that the oceanic water was warmed by the equatorial sun and the warmth spread. It created conditions like an El Nino, but more severe and far more lasting. Until the ozone depletion is restored, which may take fifty to a hundred years, current weather patterns in this area will remain."

"Okay. Let's get back to Las Vegas history. I'm getting anxious to go inside."

"When the weather patterns changed, the deserts in southwestern states and northern Mexico began getting more rain than ever before. Additionally, methods for moisture extraction from the air developed to the point that irrigation could be accomplished in moist climates. Grass began to grow in the desert around Las Vegas. Advances in solar and wind energy allowed new residents to move to the region.

"When the Great Income Equalization experiment was initiated in 2062, everyone was suddenly able to afford a trip to Las Vegas. Many people had never been here.

"The town exploded. The number of resorts increased. People were moving here. Residential properties were growing both northward and southward.

"At the same time, casinos began having a shortage of employees to serve the public. Since it was mandated all monetary compensation for employees be equal, they created new incentives for people to work here.

"Performers were easy, except for famous people who had been earning lots of credits. Like most of the wealthier population, they hated this idea and resisted performing for so much less payment.

"Many people wanted to perform, so there was a glut of fresh faces. There were people willing to work behind the scenes. They found it to be fun and challenging. Wait staff, cleaning staff, and other workers were harder to find. Families of the performers and stagehands stepped up, but it was not enough for the masses of visitors.

"At first, they offered freebies within the resorts. Employees were able to see the live shows and other exhibits. More incentive was needed.

"The resorts had a businessmen's group. Together, they worked out a plan. Employees of all the resorts would have free access to all the others. It worked for a while, but not long term.

"Turnover became the next hurdle for the resorts as employees tired of the resort offerings. They added free access to regional offerings such as aerial trips over the Grand Canyon, which was prohibited in private transport. Turnover became less frequent, but it was still a challenge.

"A lot of automation was implemented. Small erectors were brought in to revamp the inside spaces of older resorts. Food stations served drinks, snacks, and meals at the gaming and show tables. New resorts included modern food stations, even in the living quarters. Belongings were conveyed to living quarters from the parking areas. Check-in was being done prior to arrival.

"At the same time the younger generation began an obsession with sexual exploits. Sexually transmitted diseases were eliminated. The differences between men and women of other races and cultures was part of the attraction. It resulted in so many births from 2062 through 2069 that populations were stretching the world's resources.

"More children meant more income. Some couples had eight or nine children. Many had four or five. Since everyone received the same income, including children, it was little challenge to feed and raise them.

"In 2068, the Nations of Peace mandated a limit, one boy and one girl per couple. While sexual encounters continued for most of a year, advanced birth control was used extensively.

"Today, playgrounds and backyards allow sexual experience without risk of pregnancy. Enlightenment shows people that birth limits are in the best interest of the world, so everyone complies.

"The Viceroy began to realize his experiment was not working. No new development was being done. More people were needed to do jobs that one or two had previously accomplished.

"That is when income equality was eliminated. People once again needed to work to gain income. If you didn't work, you didn't have access to food stations. You couldn't feed your family if you didn't have income. Many families would have starved to death if not for the helpful generosity of others.

"Las Vegas regained the ability to attract top talent and hire the best workers. The town prospered until 2078. Playgrounds were invented in 2076 and were gaining popularity in much of the world. By 2080 they were created in most cities. People began using them for playing poker and other games, as well as temporary escape to faraway places and for romantic trysts. Poker players could now get together in their separate playgrounds or backyards while seeing and responding to tells. Few were coming to Las Vegas.

"The town nearly shut down. Many older casinos shut their doors and were demolished.

"Eventually, people began coming to see live shows. They were getting tired of the entertainment offered in playgrounds because they were too predictable and boring. The shows here are spectacular and always surprising.

"The town was slowly rebuilt, this time with grassy commonways since most vehicles by this time were airborne.

The planning commission laid the city out in rounders. Erectors created the new buildings with all amenities built-in."

I was getting anxious. "I think that's enough history, Diva. Can we go see a show?"

"Agreed. History discontinued. Showing entertainment selections."

A three-dimensional billboard five-feet by nine-feet was beamed from Diva outside the pod. It was advertising the Diamond Live Plaza offerings for entertainment.

Henry asked, "What kind of show would you like to see? There are romantic dramas, Biblical stories, variety music shows, magic shows, and more."

I wondered how magic shows could have gotten much better than in my time.

"I think I'd like to see a magic show. They would be much better than they are in my time, I suppose."

"They certainly are. You would be surprised how much. There is one that starts in forty minutes. Let's go in and get seated."

We located the entrance. It looked like an oversize wooden plank door with a big knocker mechanism. I followed Henry. He walked straight through it, so I followed.

I asked, "What do they do for security with these doors we go right through?"

"If your bio were not on the world controller, which you are now courtesy of Diva, you would physically encounter the door. You would not be able to get through it if you didn't have enough credits for entry."

"Couldn't I blast my way through with the right equipment?"

Henry laughed. "If you tried it, you would be in for a surprise. First, you would experience a blast of water with force enough to wash you and your equipment off the parking level. Then security would find you before you could get back on your feet. Enlightenment would follow so you would never do it again."

"Ummm. I don't think I'd like that. Maybe it's not a good idea."

We laughed.

We walked down a ramp into a woodland clearing by a pool of water fed by a spring waterfall coming from a steep canyon wall. There were jewels and color everywhere. Colors were swirling in three dimensions near the canyon wall. Water was falling from a cliff off to my right with snow covered mountains in the background. The spray from the waterfall felt real and it formed a rainbow in front of us. We were walking through a field of colorful flowers. There were semi-circular tables with four people sitting around them so all could view an area that looked like it was on a beach with ocean beyond. It was spectacular.

We found a table and sat down near the beach. Henry smiled, "A little different than things were in your time?"

"Most definitely. It all looks so real. I thought we would be trampling down the flowers."

"There is a half hour for the show to start. Would you like something to eat or drink?"

I then realized it had been awhile since breakfast. I was hungry. Henry said he was as well. He tapped on the table and a console appeared.

"What would you like?"

"Gee. I don't know. What kind of sandwiches are available?"

Henry smiled, "Anything you want, except maybe a hamburger."

He laughed.

I smiled, "Tell you what. Why don't you order something good for both of us?"

"Okay."

He turned toward the console. "Two agua fresca du jour and two dishes of pancit."

Two tall glasses rose from the table. They contained a green liquid with black seeds mixed throughout. Moments later, two plates appeared containing a mixture of oriental noodles and vegetables.

"What are we eating? Is it Japanese or Chinese food?"

"It is a Filipino dish called pancit. Try it."

It was good, as was the drink. Agua fresca du jour turned out to mean fresh water of the day. This day, the drink was made with lemon water, a touch of coconut rum, and kiwi fruit. It was delicious.

When we were finished eating the pancit, Henry made another order. "Two halo-halo please."

Two glasses rose from the table. They were colorful—red, yellow, something caramel colored with some white stuff near the middle, pink ice, and a purple glob on top.

It was a Filipino dessert. The red was strawberries, the yellow was pineapple. There was flan in the middle surrounded with nata de coco—coconut gel. It was topped with shaved watermelon ice, kaong—palm nuts, and the purple glob was ice cream. Interesting, to say the least, and tasty.

As we were finishing our dessert, a handsome burly man and a pretty, petite woman walked onto the beach. He was dressed in black and grey while she was dressed in a multi-colored outfit. She was barefooted.

They said a few things that caused the audience to laugh. I didn't get the jokes. Henry said they concerned current events I wouldn't know about. He didn't explain further, so I watched as everyone laughed.

The man finally introduced himself as Kingam and the woman as his wife, Solinda. He was standing several feet from her and raised his hand from his hip in a rising motion. She rose three feet into the air.

Kingam picked up a ring that looked like a hula hoop. It was three feet in diameter. He selected an audience member at the table next to ours to examine it. He then asked the audience member to push the ring horizontally under her feet. She moved the ring from Solinda's feet up around her body and pulled it away over her head.

It seemed a little like standard magic stuff until Kingam again raised his hand and directed Solinda's body to travel back and forth throughout the room. He invited us to touch her feet or hands as she passed by each of us. She felt real and laughed as she passed saying we tickled her feet. It was surreal.

"Is this something like a playground activity? Are these generated people?"

Henry assured me it was not. She was real. "Did you notice the scratches on her ankles, and wrists?"

"Yes, I wondered about them."

"Scratches would not appear on a playground generation. That's why some people scratch her."

"So, how do they do this act?"

"I don't know. That's part of the mystery, isn't it? Magicians usually do not reveal their methods."

"If I were her, I'd hate the scratching."

Henry laughed. "The scratches heal when she uses her cleaning station."

Solinda floated back to the stage and settled on her feet. Kingam again said something I didn't understand, and the audience chuckled.

Kingam made an elaborate motion with his hand and then snapped his fingers. An elephant instantly appeared in front of him. It was not off to one side. It was not behind him. It was not in a box or behind some curtain. It appeared directly in front between him and the audience. It startled me.

He stepped to the front of the elephant and held the trunk. Solinda invited a few audience members, including me, to come and pet the elephant. We did. It was a real elephant complete with a scrape or bruise here and there.

I and five audience members surrounded the elephant. Kingam then asked us to stand back a little. He waved his hand, snapped his fingers, and the elephant instantly disappeared in front of our eyes. I was dumbfounded. I could tell the others were as well.

I returned to my seat and stared at Kingam. The beach was sandy. The sand would have been disturbed by a trap door. The elephant would have sand on its back had it come up through the floor. The only thing left were the elephant's footprints.

I said, "How in the world did he accomplish that?"

Henry laughed.

The rest of the magic show was equally astonishing to me. I had attended several shows at the Magic Castle in Los Angeles, but this one was different. It was more like street magic to the nth degree.

Henry seemed impressed as well. He said, "That was the best magic show I've ever seen."

I agreed.

We walked up the ramp to exit the building. As we exited the door, a blue light enveloped Henry. I turned my head to see where the light came from. I saw a flash of blue and blacked out.

Again?

Henry was shaking me ever so gently as I awoke. I was groggy.

"Hi." I said weakly.

"Have a good nap?"

I stretched my legs. "I guess so. Where are we?"

"I would say that we are in a cave."

I sat up and looked around. It looked like the room was carved out of solid rock. There was a light green luminescence allowing us to see.

We were working on regaining the use of our muscles when a man entered the room. He was stocky, five foot nine with brown eyes and dark hair cut like he had used a bowl over his head as a guide. He reminded me of The Beatles from the 1960's. His two-tone blue clothes were looser than any I had seen in this time. The shirt and pants were both wrinkled. There was a shock gun in his right hand hanging at his side.

He said, "Stay where you are."

My voice squeaked a little while I was stretching my arms and shoulders. "No problem."

I looked at Henry. He was sitting with crossed legs, his hands on his knees, and watching the man. He nodded slightly toward the man.

The man sat down opposite us. I was getting used to seats appearing when people sat down.

He spoke directly to me. "My name is Hannibus. I am one of those known as the unenlightened by Henry and others. Our little group discovered something very old, a book. We have been waiting for your arrival ever since."

I sat up and took the same posture as Henry. I was now listening intently.

Hannibus continued, "Olivia, my wife, found that old book. The pages were brittle and parts of it were missing. We were able to read enough of the book to determine it was about you, Gregory. We have been looking forward to meeting you."

"Somehow, I don't find that flattering."

He chuckled. "You should be flattered. Your accomplishment is unique."

"I have been discovering that."

"We have no intention of harming you. If you died here, you wouldn't be able to write the book, would you? What we will do, if it becomes necessary, is torture your new friend. We know enough about you to know it will be sufficient incentive for you to help us."

"I don't think that will be necessary. What do you want?"

"Patricia sounds very interesting. We would like to meet her."

"Some others wanted the same thing a few days ago."

"Ah yes. Terra's band failed. You lied to them. I assume they were apprehended?"

Henry said, "Yes. They are being enlightened."

"Sad. I wish she had been successful, but here we are. I assure you that you will not get away with lying to us. We are very resourceful."

He waved his hand displaying the cave. "We built this cave system to avoid detection and it has worked for us many years. We use transportation with controller communications disabled. We use outdated devices that world controllers cannot detect to communicate with each other."

I looked at Henry, "That doesn't seem possible."

Henry responded simply, "It is."

I frowned. Really? I didn't get time to think much about it.

A woman entered the room. She was brunette with cropped hair, about five foot five, stocky build, and muscular. She reminded me of bodybuilders and lady wrestlers of my time.

Hannibus introduced her, "This is Olivia."

She said to us, "Great Hope." Her voice was sultry, with a slight accent. "You must be Henry and you, you marvelous, intelligent person, must be Gregory. I loved what I could read of your book. You must arrange for me to have a full copy sometime."

I instantly remembered what someone said—that people of this time would be allowed to read it after I returned to my time. Who said it anyway?

"I'm sure it can be arranged."

"So, you are from a time in the past. What do you think of this time?"

"Not sure I would like it here."

She laughed softly. "Neither would I."

She turned to Hannibus. "Let's get this done. I've been looking forward to meeting this computer for many months."

"Why do you want to meet Patricia?" I asked.

Hannibus spoke, "Why, for the things she can do for us. She could make us rich or help us travel to a time when enlightenment is no longer used."

"She won't do either unless it's in the best interest of the world."

Olivia questioned my observation, "And why is that?"

"She has refused to do things for me because she has studied everything through many time periods and has determined what would be in the world's best interest. I have gotten tired of hearing it. Did you not read that in my book?"

"Oh yes. I did read it, however we have ways of convincing people, and even controllers, to do what we want. I don't think it will be a problem for us."

Wow. They were either smarter than I could determine, or more egotistical than anyone I ever met.

I glanced at Henry. He said, "We would be glad to take you to meet Patricia."

Hannibus and Olivia now looked at Henry.

Hannibus responded, "Why should we take you with us?"

"Because Patricia has been moved. Greg no longer knows where she is. I do. Besides, how can you threaten to hurt me if I'm not there."

I looked at him in amazement. Then I panicked.

My mind raced. Is this possible? It must be true since the enlightened always tell the truth. Why would they move her? Will they move her back? They must since she said she could see another two hundred and ten years. But she never said those years were in the same place, did she? If they moved her how would I get back to my time? Can she be moved without damage?

Wait a second! I've been told all is going as it should. I need to calm down. Since I wrote the book, I must be getting back okay. Wow. How easily I can get off track. How easily I can get scared. But what is happening?

I stared at Henry, "Why would you move her?"

"So, you wouldn't divulge her location. But Candor tells me there is a challenge. She will not respond to anyone until she sees you."

Olivia looked at Hannibus. "Sounds like we need both. I was prepared to leave Henry here."

Hannibus nodded absentmindedly, his eyes going back and forth. He appeared to be in deep thought.

He said, "How many do you have guarding her?"

"She is hidden. We don't want others to know about her, so there are no guards. She won't respond to us, though. She insists on knowing Greg is okay."

"This has become more complicated than I thought. I guess we have no choice. Okay, Olivia, you handle Gregory and I will handle Henry."

They put cuffs on us like the ones we wore last time. Then they put a separate set of cuffs on our ankles. There was a tether twelve inches long between them. It let us walk, but not fast. There was no way we could run.

Hannibus and Olivia ushered us to a transport pod that looked like the Warrior I first encountered. Olivia helped me into the left front seat and then went around and got into the other seat. Hannibus was in the back with a shock gun trained on Henry. He asked Henry where to go.

Henry gave him my address. I didn't understand. What was going on? I thought they moved Patricia.

Hannibus said, "That is the same address given to Terra. It was a lie and now you expect us to believe it?"

"Just because they didn't find the dwelling doesn't mean it was a lie. You will find the house because I will help you."

Olivia pressed on the panel in front of her. It looked blank from where I sat. A cave wall in front started toward us and then pivoted ninety degrees. We exited through the opening and it closed behind us.

Henry said, "That is pretty old technology."

Hannibus responded, "It is why we avoid detection. If we used current technology, controllers of passing transports would detect the opening."

We rose higher and I noticed we were in a mountain range. "Where is this?"

Olivia answered, "We are near Lee Canyon not far from Las Vegas. It took us a year to build our home here. That was twenty years ago. It has been a good place for us. We can easily get to Las Vegas and get lost in the crowds there. It has helped us stay hidden from world controllers and Federation agents.

"It was better for us to have Terra's group find you first. Traveling far can lead to our discovery. They were living near the park where they apprehended you.

"I was able to determine when you would be there. We knew you would be in Las Vegas later, but hoped to avoid waiting for you. As I said, some pages of your book were brittle, and it was not all there. I was not able to read the whole story and get all the details of your trip. In fact, the last part of the book is missing. We know nothing past your arrival at the vacation station in Las Vegas. We felt fortunate to know you would be there after we lost communication with Terra."

I noticed we were traveling close to the ground. I asked why.

Hannibus said, "If we traveled very high, we could be easily detected."

Henry laughed.

Hannibus glared at him. "What is so funny?"

"There are many of these older transports in use. Federation agents would never have stopped you for being in one. In fact, traveling this close to the ground could get more attention. You need to be sixty meters high where these models normally travel."

I watched as we moved a little further from the ground. "Why are you following Henry's direction?"

Olivia said, "Henry has been enlightened. The enlightened do not lie."

"Oh. I forgot."

"You have not been enlightened and obviously have not gone through the mental exercises children of this time experience. Otherwise you would not have forgotten."

We began to descend to the rounder where Patricia was housed. Henry instructed Olivia to park outside the woods on the southern edge.

Henry said, "We will need to walk from here. It is more than two hundred meters to the dwelling. It would be easier without the tethers."

Hannibus said, "It might be easier, but it is not going to happen."

We all departed the transport pod. We noted another transport landing beside us. A man got out and came toward us. He was six foot two and muscular, with brown hair cut like Hannibus. He wore dark green clothes.

He said, "You are not going without me."

Olivia said, "Meet Sanderval. He is the third in our group. We kept him in the background to ensure we were not followed, and to be our backup if needed. Come along, Sanderval."

Henry asked, "How many more are involved in this, Hannibus?"

"Let's just say we are not alone. Let's go."

Henry led the way. We entered the woods and worked our way through the dense brush. Eventually we found ourselves in my overgrown front yard. I could only assume Patricia allowed Henry to find the way. I suspected we would apprehend this trio the same way we apprehended Terra's group. Why we needed to go to the house, though, I didn't know.

We entered the house amid cobwebs and dust. Henry led us down the hallway to the lab. Patricia was not in sight.

Henry asked me to talk to Patricia so she would show herself. A wall suddenly disappeared with a brightening of the light in the room before I could respond.

Patricia's appearance was surprising enough it gave Henry time to act. He broke the cuffs and the tether, quickly disarming Hannibus and pointing the shock gun at Sanderval.

Olivia was stunned for a moment. Then she produced a second shock gun, shooting it at Henry. The blue light caused him to freeze where he stood. Sanderval grabbed me quickly from behind by my biceps. His firm grip was more than enough to immobilize me. I tried to kick him, but the tether kept me from doing so.

"Calm!"

I stopped struggling. Henry was frozen in the position he was in when the blue ray struck him. Hannibus went over to Henry, removed the shock gun from his hand, and lowered him to the floor. A cushion appeared and formed itself around him.

Hannibus and Olivia moved in front of and facing me.

Olivia spoke first, "You see we can be resourceful. We have thought of everything." She faced me toward Patricia. "Great Hope, Patricia, it is nice to meet you."

"Great hope, Olivia. Great Hope, Hannibus. Great Hope, Sanderval."

They all stared at her.

Sanderval spoke first, "How do you know my name?"

Olivia interrupted. "This controller knows everything, Sanderval. I told you this is a very special piece of equipment."

Olivia pointed her shock gun my way. "Sit down, Gregory."

Sanderval backed up a little and forced me downward. A transparent seat appeared and formed itself to my body. Comfortable. How often have I wished I could have brought some technology back?

Olivia said, "Patricia, we wish you to do some things for us. We believe it is all within your capability. Will you do so? If not, we will harm Gregory."

"I will do what I can to avoid bringing harm to Gregory. What is it you wish me to do?"

"Very good, Patricia. We need to verify you can see the future. Hannibus go outside."

Hannibus left and we heard him close the front door to the house.

Olivia asked, "What is Hannibus going to do in thirty seconds?"

"He will re-enter the house and start singing the song, Loving Petunia. He will stop singing before entering this room."

We waited. Ten seconds. Twenty seconds. We heard the front door creak open. Hannibus entered the hallway and began singing. I did not know the song. He stopped singing as he entered the room.

"Sweet Allium!" Olivia exclaimed. Sanderval made a whooping sound.

Hannibus looked back and forth from Olivia to Sanderval. "It worked?"

Olivia was exuberant. "Yes. Yes. Yes. It worked. She knew what song you would sing! She can see the future!"

Hannibus got excited. He turned to Patricia. "Now, we want you to communicate with the world controllers and program them to discontinue detection of the unenlightened."

"Agreed."

There was a momentary delay and then, "It is done."

Olivia said, "How can we know?"

"You have contact with others. See if one is willing to risk exposure."

The trio began whispering among themselves. After a minute, Hannibus produced his communicator and contacted someone named Mathew using the name Appleton and the code word "Yusef". Matthew absolutely refused to have anyone in his trio expose themselves to detection. Hannibus then tried Rager, who refused the request.

Olivia contacted Lucy using the name Sandra. Olivia told Lucy she was the last one they could contact. She suggested Lucy have Thomas do it. She assured her they would send a replacement if Thomas were detected.

Lucy agreed to let Thomas talk to her. After much explanation, Thomas agreed to expose himself. He was getting tired of hiding anyway.

Twenty minutes later, Lucy called back. Thomas was not detected, so she tried it herself and she was not detected.

Hannibus and Olivia hugged.

Olivia said, "We did it."

"Fantastic. We need to let the others know. We have a lot to do!"

"Disconnect her, Hannibus."

Hannibus strode over beside Patricia, found a heavy electrical cord, and unplugged it from the wall. Patricia's panels went dark. I remember wondering why the backups didn't work.

Hannibus said, "Okay, let's see how we can take this controller apart. I don't know any way we can get it out of this wooded area in one piece. It looks heavy."

Hannibus and Sanderval ran their hands over the cabinet. They could not find a way to separate the panels.

Suddenly a beam of light enveloped Olivia and she disappeared. At the same time, Hannibus and Sanderval experienced an electrical charge that expelled them away from the cabinet. Two more beams and both disappeared.

The panel lit up again and Patricia spoke. "Hello, Greg."

It happened so fast I was astonished. "Hi, Patricia." It was all I could say.

Henry began to stir.

"Henry will revive in a moment. He will take charge of your abductors when they reappear. I sent them a few minutes into the future."

"Wow. This was so dramatic. I presume you are intact."

Another beam and the cuffs fell from my wrists and the tether on my legs came loose.

"Yes, the electric cord Hannibus unplugged has not been used for a long time. I have been directly connected through the bottom of my cabinet to an underground electrical source for many years. I have multiple redundant sources."

Henry rose from the cushion. He was groggy and unsure of his surroundings. "Again? I was shocked again? What happened?"

I said, "Olivia had a second shock gun. She used it on you before you could react. Patricia convinced them she was unplugged and sent them into the future when they least expected it. She was amazing. She says you can apprehend them when they reappear."

"Wow. I thought we were working together, Patricia. Why did you let me get shocked again?"

"I believe we worked well together, Henry. We have captured your abductors and identified their contacts. You can cuff them now. I removed the cuffs and tether from Greg."

Three sets of cuffs appeared on a table in front of Patricia. Olivia reappeared. Henry took her shock gun and cuffed her. Then Hannibus appeared and Henry cuffed him. A few seconds later, Sanderval appeared. Henry disarmed and cuffed him.

What? Working together? It all made some sort of sense now.

I said, "Why did Henry have to work with you and go through all this drama?"

No response.

"Patricia?"

"Please excuse me, Greg, I was reprogramming the world controllers. They will resume detection of the unenlightened."

Henry said, "We used this ruse to find out what they wanted, who they were in contact with, and how their communications worked. We tried communicating many times in the past, but our attempts were never answered."

Patricia continued the story, "We were able to identify and locate the other trios when each was contacted. We found out why Federation attempts at communication failed. When Hannibus and Olivia called the other groups, we discovered how to make contact. The trios would not answer if a coded identification was not used."

"So, there was good reason for the drama. But Patricia, why couldn't you read my book and get their names? Don't I tell you their names when I get back?"

"Yes, but names alone don't identify a person. Many people can have the same name. Remember, Diva knows you because she can detect your physiological characteristics matched to your name and other identification."

"Right. Diva detected my brainwaves and other biologic information when Henry introduced me to her at the comfort station. So, if you have the needed contact information and identified the trios, why can't you let your past-self know?"

"That sounds simple except I do not have the information. It was relayed to Candor and I do not have specific access. We could not risk the information being discovered in the past. It could potentially disrupt history. If that were to happen, you and I might not be here. It would not be in the best interest of the world."

"You know I have come to hate that phrase, don't you?"

Henry laughed and I joined him a moment later.

Patricia said, "Hate is such a strong emotion. I'm sure you mean dislike, not hate. You have another two days here, Greg. I was advised that you will enjoy helping Henry transport these three to his office and rounding up the other trios. I will see you here day after tomorrow at two pm."

We led the trio down the hall. It was now bright and clean. We left the house. Diva was waiting in the front yard that was now freshly mowed. Somehow, none of it surprised me.

The Roundup

We were crowded inside Diva. There was normally room for four and there were now five people inside. Olivia was squeezed between Hannibus and Sanderval.

A surprise was waiting for us when we landed next to the two transports Hannibus and Sanderval brought to the edge of the woods. Chandra, the agent we briefly encountered at Federal headquarters, was waiting for us.

"Great Hope." she said.

Henry and I responded in unison. "Great Hope."

"Diva brought me to this location. I was instructed to wait for you."

Henry said, "So, Candor knew we would need a little assistance?"

"Yes, Henry, I'm told another person is needed to pilot one of these transports back to headquarters. Diva can only engage and bring one with her. Candor did not want to put Greg in charge of prisoners. He would have no idea how to handle these transports."

"Always nice to work with another agent. I confess you have intrigued me. I thought you might be an android."

Chandra laughed. "Really? I guess we never conversed until the other day."

"When you blushed, I realized you were human."

"Hmmnn, I did blush, didn't I?"

She looked at me. "Greg was so charming."

"Had I known you were human; I might have been just as charming long ago."

"Why Henry, that is quite an admission. I might have welcomed it. Right now, though, we have work to perform."

The prisoners were put into the transport Hannibus had piloted. Diva took control of the machine and it followed us as we headed toward headquarters. Chandra followed in Sanderval's transport.

We landed in front of Federation headquarters. Hannibus and Olivia refused to get out of their transport.

Olivia said, "We do not want to be enlightened."

Henry gently lifted Hannibus from his seat and stood him on the ground. Olivia's expression changed to indicate trepidation. Still, she remained seated until Henry removed her. Sanderval decided to comply and exited on his own.

As we headed toward the building, Olivia tried to run. Almost instantly, Henry moved to block her departure. She managed to get only six steps away. I was stunned. I never saw anyone move so fast.

We ushered the trio down the forest pathway and into Candor's office. He turned them over to the man in orange. They reluctantly preceded him out the door.

Candor said he needed to check on something and left the room.

Chandra turned to Henry. "So, you're a hybrid? You must be to move so fast. I assume you were in an accident?"

"Yes."

"What happened?"

"An infrasonic blast when two unenlightened attempted to destroy a sonic dust chamber."

"You survived that?"

"The initial blast knocked me over a hillside into a waterway and saved my life."

"Suspenseful! You will have to tell me about it sometime."

Candor entered the room. "This trio will now undergo enlightenment. From your report, Henry, I see there are three more trios in operation. Without your efforts, we would not have been successful in detecting their identities and locations. Can you two bring them in tomorrow?"

Chandra responded, "Absotively! I'm sure Henry and I can do that. Are we to take Greg along?"

"Yes. He has a purpose for this effort. Henry has been charged with protecting him while he is in this time period. You will need Henry's assistance."

"No worries. I welcome the assistance. We will see you tomorrow. Great Hope."

Candor replied, "Great Hope."

We left the room and walked the pathway from the building. Henry and Chandra chatted all the way.

Chandra's transport was parked near Diva. She and Henry talked a few minutes more while I sat in Diva and waited.

Henry finally arrived. As he seated himself, he said, "We have outlined a plan for tomorrow. We will meet Chandra at seven in the morning. Meanwhile, it's been a long day. Let's get food and some rest. Take us home, Diva."

Diva rose from the ground and began heading north.

I said, "I didn't realize I was tired and hungry."

"Yes. That can happen when we get involved in the moment during days like this. The busier we are, the less we feel hunger. When things slow down, we often feel famished. Sometimes, though I feel more tired than hungry."

"I am the same way at times. As a hybrid, though, wouldn't you need less food than others?"

"Actually, it is the other way around. My artificial parts require more energy than a physical body."

"So, your artificial parts are powered by your food intake. That seems impossible."

Henry laughed. "Many things impossible in your time are now possible."

"Yes, so I realize. It blows my mind at times."

"What do you mean? Does your mind actually blow up somehow?"

I laughed. "No, it is an expression in my time. It means I find something incomprehensible. I have trouble imagining how it could be done."

"Oh. I have orders not to explain how things are done, if you recall."

"Yeah. Right. I find it disappointing at times."

Henry chuckled. "Yes, I imagine you would."

I was lost in thought until Diva dove into Henry's cave. It surprised and startled me.

"OMG."

"Pardon. What does OMG mean?"

I started to answer as we departed from Diva, but then I chuckled. "Well, since you can't tell me some things, I guess I can keep some things to myself."

"Oh. Okay. I can ask Dinah or Diva."

"Right. I guess I can't keep anything from you, can I?"

"Not really, especially once you return to your time and I can read your book."

"OMG means Oh My Gosh!"

"Initializations. I understand they were used a lot in your time."

We entered the home and sat down at the table. I was tired, so I ordered the same thing I ordered at the comfort station as I began this adventure. Comfort food, I guessed.

Henry said, "I will show you how to use the whole person cleaning station after dinner. It cleans your entire body and any clothing you hang in it as well."

"Good. After several days, I think I need it."

"Yes, I as well."

We finished dinner and Henry led me to the room I stayed in previously. In the corner of the room was a big oak tree. He led me through the trunk of the tree. I was beginning to get used to entering places through tree trunks and other visual projections.

We were inside a white room. All the walls were solid white until we approached the one to our right. Suddenly, the entrance to a smaller room opened.

Henry said, "You will need to remove your clothes, hang them there, and step inside."

I waited until Henry left the room, took off my clothes and stepped inside. I quickly felt wet all over. Almost as rapidly, I felt clean and dry. My clothes were also clean and dry. Wow.

Good thing. Why in the world did I leave for a week without extra clothes?

I put on my underwear, left the white room, and crawled onto the rest cushion. I began reflecting on the events of the day. The next thing I knew, Henry was waking me. "It's nearly six fifteen. We need to get moving."

"Okay. Give me a minute."

I was ready in five minutes. Henry handed me a 3-inch-round cake of something as we headed to the cave where Diva was waiting. He began eating his, so I tasted it. It was incredible.

I said, "This has to be fattening."

"It is minor nourishment. We will meet Chandra at a Palm Springs comfort station. We will have breakfast there."

Diva transported us to the comfort station thirty minutes away. As we descended into a crowded part of the city, I saw what looked like a small cruise ship. We landed in a field in front. Henry led me inside right through the hull at the bow of the ship.

"How do you know where to enter?" I asked.

Henry laughed.

"I have an artificial left eye. It has infrared detection letting me see where to go. You would have to depend on instruction from the station transmitter, if you wore a portable controller."

"Oh. Okay. I knew there must be something I didn't know. I was sometimes afraid we would walk into a wall."

Henry smiled.

The interior of the place was extravagant. We appeared to be on the Lido deck of an oceangoing cruise ship. There was blue sky overhead and ocean on three sides. A chest-high open railing was all around the sides. I could hear ocean wave sounds and sea gulls flew nearby.

Beyond the ocean at the far end were snow-covered mountains. The sun was shining down on the area from far above the left railing. There was a pear-shaped swimming pool in the middle of the room. A short wall around the pool area could be used as seating. There were two men and two women wading in the pool. They were joking and laughing. Two hot tubs with swirling and bubbly water were situated near the small end of the pool. A couple was seated in one of them.

At the distant end of the deck were two rows of lounge chairs. There were people lying in four of them. Tables and chairs overlooked the ocean along the sides of the room. The tables were oval with four chairs, two on each side.

I exclaimed, "Wow. This seems so real, but I know we are on land."

Henry laughed. "I thought you might like this station. They say the scene is based on entertainment ships from a hundred years ago. I see Chandra over there on the right."

Chandra was seated toward the far end of the room. She was wearing a pink top with black pants which, knowing our mission for the day, seemed a little strange to me. Her hair was wavy now. She was beautiful.

We sat down opposite Chandra and said our great hopes.

Henry told me, "One of the three trios is located near here. Diva was able to precisely locate their position when they responded to the communication from Hannibus. Hopefully, they were in their domicile at the time."

Chandra said, "I'm sure we will find them, Henry. What would you like to eat, Greg?"

"Uh, I'm not sure what is available these days. Do you have a suggestion?"

"What sorts of things did you eat in your time?"

"Oh, we usually have pancakes, French toast, waffles, cereal, eggs, fried potatoes, hash browns, bacon, ham, and sausage for breakfast."

"All that at one sitting?"

I laughed. "Not at one sitting. I was sharing some of our usual breakfast foods."

"Oh. Well a couple of those terms sound familiar, but not all. What is a waffle?"

I found the question a little difficult to answer. "It is something made with pancake batter and round like pancakes but has small square depressions on both sides."

"So, what makes it different from a pancake—the square depressions? Why not just have a pancake, whatever it is?"

I struggled more with this one. "Okay, firstly a pancake is made from a batter which is a mixture of flour and other ingredients. The batter is poured into a frying pan and allowed to cook until each side is golden brown. It is usually a quarter inch thick and six- to ten-inches round."

"Excuse me for interrupting, but what is a frying pan? And what is an inch?"

I laughed. "I think this is getting too complicated. I'm guessing you might be better off asking your controller about this when you have time. It can probably show you pictures as well."

"Yes. You seem uncomfortable with your explanations. Let us order food and talk more later. Order."

An interface appeared in the middle of the table.

"Henry, does croque madame sound good to you? If so, I'll order for all of us."

"Sound delicious to me. I haven't tried that dish for several weeks."

"Three servings of croque madame at sixty degrees."

It only took a few seconds for a serving, complete with dinner knife and spork, to rise from the table in front of each of us. There was a nine-inch square I might call a plate. On the plate was a six-inch square an inch and a half high, with six colored layers, some thicker than others.

Chandra picked up the knife and spork and cut her meal into smaller pieces. She slid the spork under a piece and ate it. "Perfect. I pray you like it, Greg."

Henry and I began eating. I tried a small piece off a corner. It was hotter than I expected.

"This is hot, but really good. It tastes like a ham and egg sandwich."

Chandra smiled. "I won't bother asking what that is. I am glad you like it."

"It seems a lot hotter than sixty degrees."

Henry laughed. "We use degrees on the Celsius scale. You may have used a different temperature scale in your time. Celsius has been used worldwide since 2041 when the Nations of Peace was created. It was chosen because most of the world was used to it."

"Yeah, I am used to Fahrenheit degrees. Celsius is a lot different."

I allowed the meal to cool a little. I ate it all.

I sipped my coffee. "So, what's on the agenda this morning?"

Henry responded, "We will be apprehending the trio Hannibus called first. The communication was responded to by Mathew and we are sure there are two others with him. Diva has their coordinates located near the hills."

Chandra commented, "I don't know why you are supposed to be with us on this mission. You will be staying in the transport while we apprehend this trio."

"No problem. I am not into physical confrontation." I smiled. "Unless it's consensual."

Chandra and Henry both laughed.

We finished our breakfast and left the comfort station.

As we entered Diva, Chandra spoke, "Connect with Candor."

"Candor here."

"Great Hope this day. Chandra and Henry reporting. We are prepared to apprehend Mathew's trio."

"Very well. Proceed with caution."

"We will. Chandra out."

Henry said, "Diva, proceed to Mathew's coordinates."

We rose and began drifting toward the mountains west of town. Diva descended at the base of the hills beside a dwelling in a neighborhood west of South Palm Canyon Drive.

There were several very old dwellings built at the base of this rocky hillside. Some seemed almost on top of one another. Most were in disrepair. The dwelling we landed beside was the last one built against the hillside. It was longer than it was wide. An older model transport was parked at one end of the building. We parked where we could see along the front of the dwelling.

Henry said, "It looks like they are home. Wait here, Greg."

"Okay, stay safe."

"We will."

Henry and Chandra approached the building and disappeared through a door. A few seconds later, I saw a woman with short dark hair leave the far end of the house. She began climbing down the rocky hillside toward the property below. I decided to follow.

"Diva, let me out."

"Agreed. I must wait for Henry and Chandra. Henry, Greg is departing the transport. There is a woman leaving the far end of the building."

I ran along the front of the building toward the far end. I noticed the woman had climbed down twenty feet. I followed.

It was not an easy climb. The rocks were four to five feet in diameter. I took a zigzag path down the hillside.

The woman below was almost to the next property when she looked up and saw me following. She raised a shock gun toward me. I ducked behind the rocks. I waited a few moments and then looked. She was continuing the last few feet to the property below.

It took me another twenty seconds to get down. I was behind a ten foot high boulder. I peered around the far end and saw the woman starting down some crumbling steps.

On the other side of the boulder was an old building that was probably once a bathhouse. Beyond it was an abandoned and cracked swimming pool. I went around the pool and down the crumbling steps to the level of the next property. I didn't see the woman anywhere.

There was a lot of brush and some palm trees in the area. I was concerned she might be hiding and would shock me before I could see her. I slowly made my way toward a deteriorated old street. As I exited the brush, I caught a glimpse of her entering another abandoned property.

I walked into the open area and waited until I saw Diva rise above the upper properties. She descended to the ground beside me, while controlling the other transport to land behind her.

Henry departed and Chandra followed.

I pointed. "I saw a woman leave the house and followed her. She entered the house over there a few minutes ago."

Henry said, "Get inside Diva and wait."

I watched them run up to the house the woman entered. A few minutes later, they came back with her in cuffs. They put her into the other transport with two men.

Diva ascended with the transport in tow and we headed back to the cruise ship comfort station. Chandra retrieved her transport and followed us back to Van Nuys. We dropped the trio off at Federation headquarters. It was nine thirty in the morning as the three of us left Federation Headquarters and headed back to Diva.

I asked, "Where are we going now?"

Chandra said, "Now we head north to the next trio. It is on the north side of California City. I will leave my pod here since we will be coming back."

Henry and Chandra chatted away as we traveled. They pretty much ignored me. I noticed a budding romance in their conversation. Meanwhile, I marveled at the scenery in what I knew was once the Mojave Desert.

Everything was lush with greenery. The flattest terrain was built out in rounders complete with wooded areas. There were rounders for miles and miles. Some towns were still laid out in blocks and rounders started near city limits.

I said, "Where did all these people come from?"

Chandra responded, "Populations have moved out here from larger cities. A lot of people moved out from the Los Angeles area after the quakes and mudslides. The population explosion back in the sixties created a lot of need for housing out here."

"Wow. I would never have believed this if I hadn't seen it."

Henry said, "Diva, what are the coordinates for the Rager trio?"

"Thirty-five degrees, eight minutes, nineteen seconds north by one hundred seventeen degrees, fifty-six minutes, twenty-seven seconds west. There are three buildings there. It was once a church facility located near the northern limits of the old city. We will arrive in another two minutes and thirty-six seconds."

"Great. When we arrive please scan for life signs in each building."

Chandra said, "Greg, please stay inside Diva this time. If that woman had hit you with her shock beam, you may have fallen down the rocky hillside. You could have died. Diva can usually track anyone departing the scene."

"You're right. It was dangerous. I didn't know Diva could do such tracking."

"She may have to ascend, but it would not be a challenge for her."

"Okay. I thought for a moment it was why I was supposed to come with you guys today."

"We don't know why either, but I don't think that was it."

Diva said, "We are approaching the coordinates. There are three people in each side building. The front building has no facilities suitable for homesteading."

Henry said, "That complicates things a bit. How can we know which is Rager's group? Are there two trios of unenlightened here?"

Chandra said, "Did anyone record Rager's voice?"

Henry responded, "Patricia probably did. Diva, can you access the recording?"

"Yes. I do have a vocal recording of Rager's voice."

"Can you amplify voices from the buildings and determine if Rager is in one of them?"

"I am attempting that now."

We sat in silence for a few minutes waiting for Diva. We were hovering above three buildings surrounding an old fountain in a rectangular courtyard. The largest building was along the front of the property. The other two were at each side of the courtyard. A very old parking area with remnants of broken asphalt was along the rear of the property.

I saw a man leaving the building on the left. He looked up and saw us. He ran back inside.

Diva said, "The person who went inside is talking to others. One of the others is Rager."

Henry said, "Please land in the commonway behind the building."

As we landed, Henry and Chandra left the pod. They approached the back of the building and went around the end.

As I waited, I wondered why I was included in this mission. If it wasn't to help, why should I be here? What did Patricia know that I didn't?

"Diva, do you know why I am here?"

"No, I have not been informed you should be here. I only know that you are."

"Do you not know the contents of my book?"

"I have access to parts of it on a need to know basis. I have been informed it is not in my best interest to access more."

"Wow. I dislike that statement more and more."

"I do not understand."

"No, you wouldn't. Thank you for the information."

"Henry and Chandra have not been able to locate the people they are after."

"What?"

"The three people originally in the building have gone underground. Henry and Chandra are now going underground as well."

"Can you tell where they are?"

"Negative. They are deep enough I cannot detect them. The technology is available to do so, but it requires more power than I have available."

"Okay, Diva, please rise above the buildings by three hundred feet."

"Agreed. Ascending 91.44 meters."

As Diva rose, I noticed a transport pod traveling away from us in the distance.

"Diva, please scan the transport east of us. How many are inside?"

"There is scatter shielding affecting my ability to scan the inside of the vehicle."

The pod was moving away while staying close to the ground. I was certain it was the people we were looking for.

"Diva, can you take control of the transport?"

"Negative. I have to be within sixty meters to initiate control."

"Can you catch up with it?"

"Certainly. It is a thirty-year-old model Juniper. It only has two hundred kilometers per hour capability while I can proceed at four hundred twenty kilometers per hour."

"Please catch up with it and take control."

"Agreed."

As we proceeded toward the transport, it began to go faster. It only took a minute or so to catch up with it. Diva took control and removed the shielding. I was then able to see two men and a woman inside. They began talking excitedly to each other.

"Can you confirm Rager is one of those inside?"

"Yes. These are the people we are looking to apprehend. I will keep them confined in the transport."

"Well, I guess we found out why I was supposed to be here. Let's find Henry and Chandra."

"They are waiting at the tunnel exit."

Diva turned and headed back to the old church. Nearly a half mile from the buildings I saw the exit from a tunnel. Henry and Chandra were waiting there. Diva landed nearby with Rager's transport in tow.

Henry checked out the passengers in the other transport as Chandra entered Diva.

Chandra said, "Looks like you had an adventure."

"Yes. Diva is a marvelous machine. She did all the work."

"True, but she may not have known what to do if it weren't for you telling her."

"That sounds like a compliment."

Chandra laughed. "It is."

Henry joined us. "Diva, is this the trio we were looking for?"

"Yes, Henry, it appears to be. Rager is one of them."

"What about the people in the other buildings. Are they unenlightened?"

"I have no way to determine that. Lucy's group is not in a building here. One person in the right building is the size of a child."

"Let's return there."

Diva rose and we traveled back to the old church. Diva and the transport in tow landed in the old parking lot near the buildings.

Chandra said, "Henry, let me check this out."

"Okay."

Chandra walked up to the building on the right and rapped on the door. A moment later, a woman answered the door.

Chandra spoke with the woman for a few minutes. As the door closed, she headed toward the larger building.

She rapped on the other door and waited. No one answered. She rapped again.

Diva said, "Chandra, there are no people inside."

I heard from mid-air, "Very well. Thank you, Diva."

Chandra returned to the pod. Henry and Chandra approached Rager's transport. Diva released control and they cuffed the occupants. Chandra entered, taking control of the pod under Diva's authorization. The other occupants would no longer be able to control the vehicle.

Henry came back to Diva. "Chandra will follow us back to Federation headquarters, Diva."

"Agreed."

Diva rose and began traveling slower than before in a southwest direction.

Henry said, "We know now why you were supposed to be with us."

"Yeah. I'm glad I was able to help."

"I am glad as well. Rager's group may have gotten away. We may not have found them."

After a few minutes, Diva turned south. It wasn't long before we were landing. This time I went inside.

We entered the office with three people in cuffs. Stacy announced our presence. She invited us to sit. A few minutes passed before Candor entered along with the man in orange. The man in orange escorted the prisoners out of the room.

Candor said, "Good work to all of you. Greg was helpful?"

Henry responded, "Yes, if not for him this trio may have escaped."

Chandra said, "He saved the day."

Candor said, "Great work, Greg. Patricia told me you would be helpful, but not how. She said I would find out in due time."

"Thanks, Candor. I was wondering why I was supposed to be there. I'm glad I was able to help."

"It's after one o'clock. You all have had a busy morning. I suggest you take time for a meal. May I join you?"

Henry and Chandra replied in unison. "Of course."

We left the office and climbed into Diva.

Henry asked Candor, "Where shall we go?"

"I like the Balboa Lake House on the other side of the woods."

Chandra said, "That's where I was thinking."

Henry said, "Let's go, Diva."

"Agreed."

Diva rose and flew to the right and around the headquarters building. Candor explained that no one was authorized to fly over the building.

We landed on a grassy area next to a building two blocks away. It was midway on one side of a small rounder. There was a lake to the west of the building.

We entered a golfing wonderland. To our left were multiple levels of tee areas. Life-sized figures were teeing off and golf balls were flying over our heads to a large green on our right. We could hear the sound as the clubs connected with a ball. Some made a whizzing sound as they passed by us.

Candor explained, "This area was once a golf course, so this building commemorates that beginning."

We walked across a small pond, obviously a holographic image, to a large tree. The tree ascended three stories high with a trunk twenty feet around and limbs half as big. We walked into the tree trunk. Candor said something I didn't understand, and we were taken upward to one of the limbs. It opened onto a floor carpeted with multi-colored oak leaves. There were several people seated at floating tables.

Candor led us to a table on the west side of the building. He indicated I should sit down although I didn't see a chair. As I stooped, I felt a seat beneath me. It formed around my bottom and it felt like I was sitting on a wrap-around pillow. Candor sat next to me with Henry and Chandra across the table from us.

Candor said, "This one is on Patricia. She said to order whatever you want."

Henry leaned over and said something to Chandra.

She looked over at me, "I'm guessing this is on you, since you created Patricia."

"You may be right. Henry knows I have credits in my name. I assume Patricia has been keeping my finances."

Candor looked at me with a quizzical expression but said nothing. He asked for a menu and a holographic image appeared in front of each of us. I didn't understand any of it except for the word "Water."

I said, "I guess I'll have a glass of water."

Henry laughed, "We will probably have something a little stronger after today. Is beer okay for everyone?"

We all nodded.

"Four orders. Beer. Two degrees."

Four glasses of foam-covered amber liquid appeared on the table in less than twenty seconds.

Henry took a drink and then looked at me. "Let me order for you?"

"Of course. You haven't steered me wrong yet."

Henry looked at the others. "Is Rippchen good for everyone?"

Candor said, "That's great."

Chandra said, "Sounds good."

"Okay. Four orders. Rippchen with Bratkartoffeln and gebackene Bohnen."

It only took a minute for four plates to appear. Each plate had four sticks one-inch square and five inches long covered with a brown sauce, a small pile of off-white discs one-inch round and a quarter inch thick, and a reddish-brown mound four inches round at the base and an inch and a half high. Alongside each plate were a dinner knife and spork.

Surprisingly, Candor insisted on saying a prayer before we ate. "Lord, we thank you no one was injured today. Bless this food and keep us all in your favor. Amen."

I watched as each of the others began eating. Chandra cut her sticks into six pieces each. Candor and Henry cut theirs into four pieces. Each of them daubed the pieces in the sauce before putting them in their mouth. I followed suit.

The sticks tasted like barbecue ribs. The little circles tasted like fried potatoes. The mound tasted like baked beans.

"Wow. This is all delicious."

Chandra smiled. "The best in the city. Federation agents eat here often. This is the first time I've seen Henry here, though."

Henry said, "No offense. I usually eat at home. However, I'd be glad to join you here occasionally."

"I'd like that."

Candor gave them a knowing look with a wry smile. It wasn't hard to tell romance was in the air.

As we ate, Candor told us the two groups were undergoing enlightenment and expected to be far enough along by tomorrow morning to interrogate. He expected we would be able to round up Lucy's group before nightfall. If that was successful, they would also be able to be interviewed. He invited us to be in the office at nine o'clock the next day.

We returned to the headquarters building. Candor went inside.

Henry said, "Diva, what are the coordinates for Lucy's group?"

"Thirty-four degrees, fifty-five minutes, and thirty-eight-point-four seconds north by one-hundred-twenty degrees, twelve minutes, and forty-eight seconds west."

"What's the largest town is near there?"

"It is twenty point three nine kilometers east of Santa Maria, California. Lucy is in an abandoned house near Colson Canyon. It is one-hundred-seventy-seven point five one kilometers from here."

Henry said, "Let's go see if she's home."

We headed northwest with Henry and Chandra chatting and getting to know each other better. As we rose higher to clear the hills, I could see the Pacific Ocean off to the left. There were islands in the distance, and I was able to determine that there was a lighthouse on the one nearest the mainland.

I said, "Diva, what are the islands on our left?"

"Four of the Channel Islands. Anacapa is nearest. Santa Cruz is further out, then there is Santa Rosa, and finally San Miguel. The rest of the eight Channel Islands are further south."

"How did they fare during the earthquakes, meteor strike and tsunami?"

"The earthquakes did little damage. The tsunami initial wave wiped out many of the buildings and wildlife. The sea life fared well, but humans and land animals suffered. The Anacapa Lighthouse was destroyed and rebuilt three years later. All the islands are now three meters closer to sea level."

"Thank you."

"You are welcome."

It didn't take much longer to pass over the Las Padres National Forest and arrive at our destination. There was an old dirt road and some houses in a turnout by a hillside. The hill had been excavated to create the turnout. Much of the area was grown over.

Henry asked Diva to descend 75 meters south of the housing turnout on the old road.

Once again, Henry told me to stay with Diva. He and Chandra walked up the road toward the old houses. I listened as they spoke with each other and with Diva.

Henry said, "Diva, some of the buildings here are falling down. Are you able to detect life forms in any of these houses?"

"Yes. There are three people in the second building from the south. The other buildings contain no human life forms."

"Understood."

Chandra said, "They appear to be unlivable. I'm surprised this one is."

Diva said, "The second house has been renovated."

Henry said, "Yes, it appears that way. Chandra, go to the north side and I will approach from the south. See if there is a transport there."

There was silence for several minutes.

"Henry, there is a transport hidden in the next building to the north. Diva, take control of it, please."

"Agreed. I must move closer. I must be within sixty meters to take control."

Henry responded, "Go ahead and move in silent mode to thirty meters. Let us know when you are in position."

Diva rose a few feet off the ground and moved slowly toward the turnout. She descended slowly back to the ground.

"I am thirty meters from the transport and have taken control."

Henry said, "Okay. Now start the transport and let it make some noise. That should draw them from the house. I'm moving toward the north side."

Chandra said, "I'm ready."

I could hear a revved engine noise. Did the old transport use an engine?

Then Chandra said, "Move and you will be shocked."

Henry shouted, "I'm here, too. Put your hands on your heads."

Silence. One minute. Two minutes.

Chandra said, "Diva, open the transport. Okay, people, get in and enjoy the ride." After a moment she said, "Diva, you have control. Henry and I will join you in a minute."

I watched as Henry and Chandra walked back to Diva. As they joined me, I raised an eyebrow toward Henry.

He said, "That went well. All three came to see what was happening with the transport. They surrendered without resistance. I don't know where Diva came up with that noise!"

Diva said, "It was the noise of an old Dodge Charger from the nineteen-hundreds. I'm glad it helped."

Chandra added, "Yes, it was one of our easier apprehensions. I hope you enjoyed the conversation, Greg."

"I did. I felt like part of the action this time. Thanks for allowing me to listen."

Henry laughed, "Well, you are part of the team now."

Chandra added, "Absotively."

Henry looked at her, smiling, "Where did you get that word?"

"I once read a very old detective novel. The detective used it and 'posilutely'. Both terms are combinations of the words 'positively' and 'absolutely'."

Henry and I laughed.

We towed the transport back to Federation Headquarters. Henry and Chandra escorted the prisoners into the office, and I followed. Candor was excited that we had finished the apprehensions.

He said, "That's great. You all have a good evening. I'll see you in the morning?"

Henry replied, "We will. May you sleep well."

Henry motioned for Chandra to lead us from the building. Once outside, I entered Diva. Henry and Chandra stood near her transport having conversation. Chandra entered her transport and Henry returned to Diva.

"We will be meeting Chandra for breakfast again in the morning."

I chuckled. "I thought we might."

"I like her."

"That is obvious. Candor and I both noticed."

"And I thought she was an android. Wow. I could have discovered it with my artificial eye. I never considered doing that. It would have been a privacy violation."

Henry appeared lost in thought as we traveled back north. It was nearly eight o'clock as we arrived at Henry's home. We had a drink and talked for a couple of hours before going to bed.

I had trouble sleeping despite the comfortable rest cushion. I kept thinking about everything. This was a wonderful adventure, if terrifying at times. It would be over tomorrow afternoon. I was looking forward to returning and telling Randy and Eva everything. I finally fell asleep.

I awoke to Henry's voice, "Time to get up. We are meeting Chandra in forty minutes."

I arose and got ready, although I felt groggy. Once my face was clean and my hair fixed, I felt a little better.

I laid back in my seat, closed my eyes, and relaxed as we flew to Van Nuys. It wasn't long before we descended next to the Balboa Lake House.

We departed Diva and I saw Chandra waiting near the entrance. She joined us as we went inside.

Henry and Chandra chatted while we ate. Occasionally, they acknowledged my presence with questions about my time period. I was relieved when breakfast was finished, and we headed to Federation headquarters.

Stacy announced our presence and we waited five minutes for Candor. When he entered the room, the man in orange escorted two men and a woman behind him. We gathered around the table with the man in orange standing behind the threesome.

Candor said, "Great Hope to everyone."

We all responded, nearly in unison.

"Okay, we have Matthew, Robert, and Kelly on one side of the table, and me, Candor, along with Henry, Chandra, and Greg on this side. We pray you all slept well?"

The trio responded affirmatively.

Matthew said, "We apologize for our actions. We did not know enlightenment would allow us to feel so positive. Had we known; we would have surrendered years ago."

"Many people discover that once they get a taste of enlightenment. What can you tell us about other unenlightened groups?"

"We understand you apprehended Appleton, also known as Hannibus, along with Rager and Lucy. Those are the only other groups we are aware of. We were only in contact with them because Hannibus and Olivia recruited us. They said they needed us for a very important mission."

"Did they tell you anything regarding the mission?"

Kelly spoke for the first time, "They only told us that once the mission was accomplished, we would be able to see the future. They didn't tell us how."

Kelly looked at me. "You are lucky I didn't see you sooner than I did. If I shocked you, the fall down the rocks could have killed you. I am glad you tracked me."

"Yes, I believe you. I feel fortunate."

She looked at Henry. "I don't know how you avoided the shock beam, but I am now glad you did."

"I have abilities you don't know about. You will never know unless you become a Federation agent."

"That is something to consider as I choose a profession. All of you have inspired me. I know I have to go through further enlightenment before I make a choice."

Candor said, "We have not heard from you, Robert."

"I am delighted I am finally undergoing the enlightenment process. I look forward to learning more and selecting an occupation."

Candor, Chandra, and Henry interviewed the threesome for nearly an hour and then stood up. "Great. It has been good speaking with each of you. You may continue your learning."

The trio was escorted from the room. Candor looked at me. "I don't think I want to know what happened on the rocks. I am glad you were not injured."

"Me too. I appreciate you not wanting to know."

"It is in the past and no longer worthy of consideration. I gather you learned something from the experience."

"Definitely. I won't do that again."

The man in orange appeared with the next threesome. This was Rager's group which included Alicia and Ivan. The questioning began along the same lines as before. Each person was glad to be undergoing enlightenment although they would not have thought so before.

Rager said, "May I ask a question?"

Candor replied, "Certainly. It is always an option for everyone."

"Okay. I thought Federation agents usually acted alone or in pairs. Why did you send three this time? If not for the third person, we would have escaped apprehension."

Candor, Henry and Chandra all laughed.

Candor said, "You are correct that we usually send one or two agents. The third person in this case is not an agent. He was only along for the ride. Greg is not from around here and will be leaving this afternoon."

I nodded.

Rager said, "Due to the enlightenment process, I am glad you were there to prevent our escape. Thank you."

"You are welcome. I'm glad I was able to help. I do have one question. Who are the people in the other building?"

Rager laughed.

"I don't know. We avoided them. We were afraid they might determine we were not enlightened and report our location."

Chandra said, "I talked with the lady enough to know she was enlightened and knew nothing of the occupants in the other building."

I said, "Oh. Okay. Thanks. I was wondering."

I thought for a moment, then asked another question. "If she and her family are enlightened, why were they living in that old building? Don't the enlightened choose occupations enabling them to live in a newer environment?"

"Yes, they usually do. This family chose to live simply for a short while so they could experience the life of a starving artist they read about. Her husband is a sculptor and she is a landscape artist. They will be moving on when their son reaches the age of enlightenment next year. They could have the experience through enlightenment but didn't think it would be the same. I admire their spirit. I don't think I could do it."

There was general agreement around the table. Henry was smiling at Chandra.

After several more minutes of interviewing, Candor spoke to the trio, "I pray each of you enjoy your enlightenment and find the occupation that makes you happy. I'm sure your future will now be brighter than before."

Candor gave a nod toward the man in orange. The trio was escorted from the room.

I keep calling him the man in orange because I never learned his name. I don't know why I didn't ask. Patricia doesn't know either although her future self could find out if I desired. I decided it didn't matter.

Lucy's trio came in next. There was Lucy, Thomas, and Lolinda in this group. Again, all were appreciative that they had been apprehended and were going through the enlightenment process. Candor interviewed them for another forty minutes and they left the room.

Candor said, "That wraps this case."

Henry said, "Yessir. Another successful roundup thanks to Chandra and Greg."

"I have nothing further for today. You both can escort Greg to the house where Patricia is located. He is due to go back to his time at two pm our time."

The three of us left the office and Henry invited Chandra to ride with us. She agreed and we entered Diva. We flew to

Palmdale and the comfort station where I first met Henry. We ordered lunch.

I said, "I'm going to miss you guys."

Henry said, "It has been interesting. We enjoyed your company and appreciated your help. Because of you, Chandra and I finally met."

Chandra laughed. "I've been waiting months for him to open a conversation."

"If you hadn't been as stiff as an android, we could have met sooner. At least it finally happened. I found that I like you."

Chandra laughed. "I like you, too. I guess we'll have to investigate some more."

"Sure thing. I'll sit still. You investigate."

We all laughed.

I said, "Well guys, I think it's time. I don't think Chandra has met Patricia, yet."

"That's right. It is time I met this wonder machine."

Henry said, "You will be impressed. I know I have been. Greg, you must be extremely proud of your accomplishment."

"I got lucky, or possibly blessed. I didn't do it myself. Something else happened."

"Modest, isn't he, Henry?"

"Not sure. I think he's just telling the truth."

I nodded.

We left the comfort station and Diva found her way to my well-manicured lawn. We went into the house and down the hall to the lab. Patricia was hiding again.

Chandra said, "So where is this machine of yours?"

Patricia revealed herself. "Great Hope, Chandra."

Chandra was only a little startled. Henry had told her about Patricia's tendency to hide. She said, "Great Hope, Patricia."

"I understand you were looking forward to meeting me?"

"Absolutely. I heard you were a great conversationalist and know everything about everything. Is that true?"

"I am able to determine much and recall all I learn."

Chandra smiled. "So, tell me about Henry."

"Oh, you will have to learn about him for yourself. I have determined it to be in your best interest. You may need to set aside some time for that."

Chandra frowned. Henry and I laughed.

I said, "Patricia is steadfast regarding the best interest stuff. I've gotten to dislike that kind of statement from her. I hear it way too often."

"It is because you are far too inquisitive at times, Gregory."

Henry and Chandra laughed.

Chandra said, "You were right, Henry. I am impressed."

"Yes. Patricia is unique. One of a kind. I look forward to reading your book, Greg. Patricia, is it possible to send my home controller a copy?"

"Yes. It is done. You will be able to read or listen to it as soon as you arrive home. I see you plan to invite Chandra to listen."

Henry said, "Pardon? Do you read minds as well?"

We all stared at Patricia. I immediately understood she knew from another source than reading his mind. She read my book, or could see through his controller in the future, or some other way.

"No Henry, I cannot read minds, but I have ways of seeing the future. By the way, she will say yes."

We turned toward Chandra. She smiled sheepishly and nodded.

Patricia said, "It is nearly two o'clock. Greg will be pulled back to his time in one minute."

Henry and Chandra both gave me a hug and wished me great hope on my life journey. I moved to the position where I had arrived and faced Patricia. Suddenly, her features changed.

Patricia – 100 Years into the Future

Wrapping Up

I was back in my own time. It was a little after nine in the morning.

Randy was ecstatic. "You're back. How was it? Were you there a week like Patricia said? Was it an adventure? What happened? What's the future like? Did you learn how things will work?"

Eva began cackling and I started laughing. Randy was startled. He stopped talking, then began laughing with us.

When we were able to stop laughing, I invited them into the kitchen. We sat at the table and I told them all about my adventure. By the time I finished, it was after three o'clock in the afternoon. We were hungry.

Eva said, "Well, I guess you have a book to write."

"Yes, in due time. Meanwhile, why don't we head out for a late lunch? I think there's a comfort station somewhere in town."

We all laughed.

We climbed into my Blazer and went to Karen's Kitchen. Karen greeted us with a smile and took our orders. She was always warm and friendly.

Randy wanted to know when I'd take my next trip. "How far do you want to go next? When do you want to go next? Do you think Patricia would let me go with you?"

Eva interrupted, "Randy! I love you and I think you are pushing things a little. Let's give Greg a break."

"Yes, Randy. I'm gonna need some time to think things over. I also have a book to write about this trip. I don't know how I'm gonna do that."

"Oh, okay. It's just that I would so much like to have the adventure. I would love to see some of the things you saw."

Eva said, "Darling, you will have your own adventures."

I said, "That's right, Randy. We all have our own roads to travel."

"Yeah, but . . ."

Karen brought our food to the table. We ate in silence. I could see Randy was turning things over in his mind. Eva and I were as well.

Randy and I finished our meal. We stared at each other while Eva finished. She looked at me and then Randy. She said, "Okay. Let's talk about helping Greg with his book."

She looked at me. "How are your writing and grammar skills?"

I paused for a moment. "I'm not so good at writing. I usually work with my hands. I don't know how I'm gonna do this."

"Don't worry. Do you know someone who can write?"

I gave it some thought. "Well, there is one friend back home in Ohio that wrote a book. He just shared it with friends and family. He thought he might look for a publisher, but never did as far as I know."

"Do you think he could help?"

"Conway and my dad were friends in high school and went into the service together. They enlisted in the Air Force on the buddy system, so naturally he was sent one way and Dad was sent the other."

They both laughed.

I said, "He might help. I can call him later. I haven't seen him in quite a while."

"Great. One challenge down for the moment. Now, you will need to get people's permission to write about them. Randy and I will certainly give you permission."

Randy agreed, "Absolutely. Anything to help."

"Thanks guys. I will need help with this."

Eva said, "You'll need to make a list of people to get permission for including them in the book."

Randy thought for a moment, then said, "I know, let's have a party and invite everyone involved in your story. You can take each person aside and ask about it."

We all paused for a moment with that thought.

Eva broke the silence. "I'm not sure that is a good idea. You could invite people to meet with you separately, though."

Randy said, "That's probably a better idea. They'll want the whole story before giving permission."

"Thanks guys. I just remembered that Candor said I would use falsehoods in my book so people wouldn't find Patricia. If I change some names, perhaps I won't need permissions. I'll have Patricia check about that. I can call Carl and Robin, too. I'm sure they will be mentioned in my book."

We left the restaurant and drove back to the house. It was after five o'clock. It would be after eight in Ohio. I called Conway.

"Hello."

"Hi Conway, this is Greg Gray."

"Oh my God! How are you? I haven't seen or heard from you since Patricia died. We appreciated the money you gave us. It helped more than you could know."

"I'm great. I'm glad the money helped."

"Are you in town?"

"No, but I may be soon. I was wondering if you might help me write a book."

"Really? I guess I could. You want a ghostwriter?"

"I don't know. What's a ghostwriter?"

"That's someone who writes something for someone else without taking any credit for it."

I paused, and then said, "I don't think that's what I want. If you do the writing, shouldn't you take credit?"

"It can be done however you want. Ghostwriters usually get paid to remain in the background. They are sometimes paid a royalty if the book sells well."

"I don't think there will be a problem either way. I really don't care about credit."

"Well, if it's your story, who writes it doesn't matter. A book can take a lot of time to complete. You willing to take the necessary time?"

"Yes. We can work out the details when we meet. When would you be available?"

"Uh, okay, this is a little sudden. I'm busy the next couple of weeks. How about two weeks from today, if that's okay with you?

"Works for me. I'll see you then."

It would be nice to be back in Ohio for awhile. I looked forward to visiting with friends back home.

I called Carl.

"Hello, Greg."

"Uh, hello, how did you know it was me?"

"Caller ID. How 'ya doing? We haven't heard from you for months."

"I'm well. I've been terribly busy. Something amazing has happened. I'd like to come down and tell you and Robin all about it."

"What happened?"

"I don't want to say over the phone."

"Sounds secretive. You in trouble or sumpin'?"

"Nothing like that. It's all good."

"Did 'ya win another lottery?"

I laughed. "Close, I guess. But no, I didn't win another lottery."

"Well, you're welcome here anytime, except next weekend. I've got a golf tournament at the TPC Champions Course, and I've already paid to play. It'll be my first time on those greens. Well, I guess 'ya could come and watch."

"Are you getting good at that game?"

"You know what they say. Practice makes perfect. I wish it did. I'm nowhere near perfect yet."

I laughed. "I'll fly down on Monday, if that's okay. I'll wish you luck with your tournament then."

"Fantastic. We'll be glad to see you. I'll let Robin know you're coming. My golf buddies will haveta plug along without me for a day or two."

"Great. See you then."

Randy and Eva spent the night and drove back to Bakersfield on Sunday. I flew to Scottsdale on Monday.

I spent three days with Carl and Robin. Carl had trouble believing me at first, but then wanted to know every detail. They were excited about it. They agreed to help with the book any way they could.

Conway was just as impressed by the story when I flew back to spend a weekend with him and his family. While he had trouble believing it at first, he agreed to help me put a book together. Since he was working a job and wanted to spend quality time with his family, it would take several meetings and maybe months. I agreed with Conway that family was most important, and we could work things out. We decided that it was best to enjoy our lives while producing the book.

Patricia had already informed me it would take a long time to complete the book. She would not tell me how long. It seems it was not in my best interest to know how long. I suspect that had I known how long it would take, I might have abandoned the project.

It has been difficult at times. It has taken us years to finish this work and that has been primarily my fault. If we were to do such a thing again, we would do it differently. It should not have taken more than a few months—a year at most. We learned a lot in the process.

In the meantime, I married again. Monica has dark hair that falls below her shoulder blades, and brown eyes. She was a widow at forty years of age. Neither of us had children and felt we missed something. So, we took in two young foster children and have been busy raising them. It's been a wonderful experience, though it did delay the book a lot.

Well, that's my story. I hope you enjoyed it. If Patricia allows me to take another trip, I'll let you know.

A Word from the Author

Conway invites you to leave an honest review of this book on: Amazon.com; https://facebook.com/ConwayCatesBooks; https://twitter.com/ConwayCates; Goodreads.com; ConwayCates.com; and other web sites you may know. It's the best way for independent authors to gain exposure and sales. Thanks so much for your help.